Flynn was on my end of the long line of players. His thick, dark hair ruffled in the breeze. He was one of the lucky guys whose cheeks actually showed it when he decided not to shave that day—very rough, very heart-stopping for the girls who got close, if not for the other team. It was so tempting to use my telephoto. But I was a disciplined journalist. Besides, when reviewing my photos from the previous year, I noticed I had zoomed in on Flynn like thirty times too many. It wasn't like I was in love with him or something—I've never even spoken to him, except to say "Hold it right there" or "Cheese." No, I had nothing more dangerous than what I call a "camera crush."

Elizabeth Chandler

Love at First Click

HARPER TEEN

AN IMPRINT OF HARPERCOLLINS*PUBLISHERS*

*T*his shot was going to be fabulous! Of course, many of the bodies in my viewfinder—all of them belonging to our high school football team—came as already, premade, just-add-flavoring fabulous. But aside from that, the sky was amazing—it looked almost painted—with the sun slicing horizontally through clouds. Muscular arms in every shade from white to dark brown shimmered with sweat. It was late August, hot and humid, a preseason practice. I knelt on the sideline, poised for a series of shots, aware that I was pushing my luck with Coach.

Coach Siefert doesn't like girls, banned them from

practices, and would have banned us from games if he could have. He considers "females" a major distraction; so maybe I should have been insulted that he allowed *me* to get as close as I did, as photographer for the school paper.

Of course, I dressed in a nondistracting way. My dark, wavy hair, which falls about six inches below my shoulders, is always braided or somehow tied down. I couldn't have it blowing in front of the camera lens. And I wore the same kind of clothes to practice and games: plain shirts, khakis pants, and athletic shoes. I love dressing girly, but on the job, I'm a professional. So it seemed to me I had earned my right to kneel on the chalky sideline—okay, maybe I was edging over it just a bit—to take the perfect shot.

I pressed the toggle switch on my digital, frowned, and tried again. "Oh, no! Nooo!"

A drained battery. How could I have let this happen? I looked over my shoulder to see where I'd left my equipment bag.

"Heads up! Heads up!" voices shouted.

I heard the thunder of feet coming in my direction, but I knelt there like a lawn ornament, glaring at my equipment. Suddenly, the camera was flying over my head. My butt landed first, then I was flat on my back. I saw the sky shining directly above me between the red helmet and padded shoulders of the heap of body sprawled on top of me. The heap was breathing hard. Sandwiched between us was a football.

The player on top of me casually rolled onto his back and stood up. He didn't seem to notice he'd landed on a body. All that padding, I guess, or he was just keeping the focus that Coach was always screaming about. I didn't blame him—I was focused on finding our very expensive school camera. Spotting it just behind me, I picked it up and cradled it in my hands like a baby, praying it wasn't damaged.

"You okay?" Jared Wright hollered. I recognized his voice; as quarterback he called all the plays. And he regularly called my sister.

"Sure," Flynn Delancy replied, tossing back the football he had just caught, grinning at the defender who had failed to bring him down.

"Not you, you moron," Jared replied, and the rest of the team laughed. "Hayley," he called to me, "are *you* okay?"

Flynn looked back and seemed surprised to see me sitting on the ground. "Oh. Sorry! Sorry, buddy," he said, taking a few steps back, extending his hand, pulling me to my feet in a single motion, like I was his teammate.

Between the red of his helmet and the metal face mask,

I glimpsed the famous eyes. Gray, but a gray that could turn mystical blue. Sometimes, they were the color of the night sky when it first lightens to silver; at other times, they were a stormy ocean.

How would I know this from shooting sports? Hey, I do close-ups! There is nothing that grabs your audience like a tight shot. And, actually, I photograph all kinds of school activities—dances, concerts, fund-raisers, and everyday moments by the lockers. With a camera in my hand, I don't feel shy. It's not *me* everyone is looking at—it's the eye of the camera; it's the people who they imagine will be admiring their photos. I like it that way. Usually.

The glimpse of Flynn Delancy's eyes was no more than a glimpse, couldn't be, not with Coach Siefert yelling like a maniac. The guys were told to "keep your focus," and I was asked, not very nicely, to leave.

As I gathered my stuff, one of the assistant coaches trotted over to ask if I was all right.

"Oh, yeah."

"You know Coach," he said, with an expression that was half smile, half grimace.

"I know Coach. I'll be back tomorrow."

I saw another half smile, half grimace on the assistant's face, this one about me, I thought.

As I headed out of the stadium, I heard a pair of feet shuffle up behind me.

"You've got grass stains on your back."

I turned around. My friend, Gabriel, who covers sports for *The Courier*, and who'd been working on the other side of the field, had followed me.

"There goes my designer shirt," I replied with a laugh.

"That's a designer shirt? I've always wondered how you can tell."

"Gabriel," I said, shaking my head, "it's a shirt just like yours, from L.L. Bean."

"It's Gabe," he corrected me, for the millionth time.

I love my friend's name, Gabriel Milano. It goes perfectly with his curly gold hair and strong features. But he has this thing about being called Gabe—it sounds tougher, I guess, more like a sportswriter, less like an Italian fashion designer. He is the best writer at Saylor Mill High, even though he's only going into sophomore year like me—he has *that* much talent. He could write anything, but he loves covering athletics.

During freshman year I started hanging with him, trying to soak up his knowledge of sports. He spent hours teaching me on the sidelines and in the gym bleachers, so that I could better anticipate the shot that would be the big one, and we had become good friends. There was nothing romantic between us, never would be, but as his good friend I knew his gentle heart, which made him Gabriel to me.

He was quiet as we walked back to the main school building, and I figured he was working on his column. Our deadline for *The Courier* is always Wednesday at four P.M., with publication each Friday. Labor Day weekend and the first two days of school should have given us plenty of time between now and the deadline, but we were battling against that kind of slow motion you feel at the end of summer.

"So do you know what your predictions will be?" I asked.

"Huh?"

"Your predictions for the football team, for the league. I thought you were going to list them in your first column."

"Yeah. Yeah, I am."

I looked at him questioningly.

"I just don't get it," he said, and sighed.

"It doesn't seem that hard," I replied. "We came in second last year and our team was young. I think we're going to bag the championship this year."

"Of course," he said. "I don't see how we can't, I mean, barring injuries."

"So what don't you get?"

"Girls."

"Oh."

"Girls and jocks," he added.

"As two separate categories or combined?" I asked, shifting my camera bag to my other shoulder. My equipment was heavy, but I'd never ask Gabriel to carry it.

"Combined. Why do girls chase jocks? Why do they think they're so great?"

I shrugged. If he had asked me why my camera loved Flynn Delancy's face, why Flynn's eyes were *made* for film, or, why, if I were Michelangelo, I would have asked Flynn to pose for *David*, I could have given an intelligent answer. But I wasn't ready to offer a theory on why girls *chased* guys like Flynn, Jared, or other jock studs. I had decided last year that they weren't worth it.

"I mean, they're such jerks," he said. The heat and humidity must have been making him grouchy.

"Well," I replied, "it's obvious that jocks can be self-absorbed and egotistical. And that makes them blind to other people—insensitive—but not exactly jerks. What I'm saying is, the stupid way they act isn't always intentional."

"Delancy would have left his cleat marks on you and never known it if someone hadn't called his attention to you."

I shrugged. "It's part of being a sports photographer."

"Carelessness, when it's continual, is as bad as intentional jerkiness."

"That's what I love about you, Gabriel, you do philosophy as well as sports."

"Ever noticed how girls chase jerks rather than nice guys?" he added.

Ah, now we were getting to what was bothering him. I had a bad feeling he'd been turned down by that girl he'd been ogling at his swim club.

We entered the school building. "Listen, Gabriel, it's ninety-something degrees, as humid as a rain forest, and I think I've got a fat bruise coloring my rump. I'm not in the mood to get depressed by the fact that girls don't chase nice sportswriters, and a jock wouldn't notice if he left cleat marks on me. I'm going to burn a CD, then work on my photos at home."

Which is what I did, pausing only for a moment, to open a file and admire a picture of Flynn.

On the way home I stopped at Marty's Camera Shop, which isn't far from school, in "the heart of Saylor Mill," as they say, that being all of about two blocks of shops and businesses. Saylor Mill is one of those places that began as the next big intersection outside of a city, tried to call itself a town, and eventually became one more suburb for people working in Baltimore and Washington.

The owner of Marty's, a tall man in his sixties, looked up as I entered. "I still got her," he told me. *Her* was a used Olympus film camera plus lenses that would have sold for eighteen hundred dollars new, and was in the cabinet with a tag of one thousand dollars. I was stashing away money, hoping Marty wouldn't sell the camera before I had enough. I poked around the shop for a few minutes, went back to admire "her," then walked the long mile home.

Our home is a one-level spread laid out exactly right for a widowed father and two teens. From the front foyer, you walk back to a family room with a cathedral ceiling and fireplace. To the left of the foyer are two bedrooms separated by a bath—my sister's and mine. To the right of the foyer was the kitchen and dining room, and beyond that, to the far right of the house, the master bedroom suite, where Dad can avoid our music and our fights over the bathroom.

"Hello, Mrs. Klein. Smells good," I lied, sticking my head into the kitchen.

She grunted and poked a fork into a potato with such force that, if it wasn't soft from cooking, it would now be soft from poking. "I told your father I am not picking up after you girls," she said. "You are too old for me to be picking up your rooms."

"Okay," I replied agreeably.

This was one of the several welcome-home greetings that Mrs. Klein rotated through. To someone else, it might seem kind of cold, but not to Breeze and me. Mrs.

Klein arrived when Breeze was four and I was three, just after our mother died from cancer. She was hired as a housekeeper, *not* a childcare provider, as she so often said, and motherliness wasn't one of her traits. But steadiness was, and when you have a sweet, loving, spacey dad who gets totally involved in his work, you come to appreciate reliability. Dinner has always been ready at six-fifteen, whether we're ready to eat it or not, and broccoli has always been cooked until it seems more like green potatoes. Without these events happening again and again in our lives, we'd all feel lost.

When I reached Breeze's and my side of the house, I saw what had prompted today's greeting. Clothes hung from Breeze's closet door and full-length mirror stand. Splashes of colorful shirts, shorts, skirts, pants, and dresses draped the bed and assorted furniture. I stepped inside the room, grinning.

"Is it a fifty percent off-everything sale?"

Breeze, whose real name is Brianna, sighed. "I'm just not inspired."

"You're trying to pick out your outfit for the first day of school," I guessed.

She held a skimpy purple skirt to her waist, then tossed it aside. "And the second and third and fourth—thank God it's only a four-day week!"

I nodded. In her clothing choices, Breeze considered much more than how stuff would look with her blond hair and green eyes (fabulous!) and how a certain top went with a pair of pants. She also thought about how Tuesday's look set up Wednesday's, how Wednesday's affected Thursday's, and how Thursday's outfit would contrast with Friday's. I admired her attention to color and texture. But I, myself, could never remember what someone wore the previous day, and I wasn't sure how many people at school truly appreciated her wardrobe compositions.

"At least there will be lots of sales for Labor Day weekend," she said.

"Lots," I replied. "A girl can never have too many clothes."

A more responsible sister might have pointed out to Breeze that she had gone *way* over the clothes budget that Dad had set for us, way over for five months in a row. But because of the way Dad manages our money, I didn't. Like a lot of parents, he is obsessed with keeping things "even." So when he looks at the credit card charges each month—we each have our own card—and sees how much Breeze has gone over, he quietly gives me that amount in cash. Which is how I bought my digital, and how I'm saving for my Olympus. Hopefully, I'll be able to buy the camera before Breeze puts us in bankruptcy.

"I'm taking a long shower," I warned her. "I may not come out for a while."

"Wait, I need my nail polish."

At that moment the phone rang. Breeze looked torn between the need to paint her nails and the desire to answer the phone.

"Want me to get it?"

"No! Yes! I don't know. I've been waiting for him to call for the last half hour. But I don't want him to think . . ." She drummed her long nails on the bedside table.

"It's on its fourth ring," I said. "The answering machine is about to—"

"Get it! Get it!" she screamed.

I laughed and dashed across her room to snatch up the receiver. "Hello?"

"Breeze?"

"Hayley."

"Haaay-ley! This is Jared."

Like I didn't know. "Hi, Jared."

"Are you okay? I've been wondering if you were okay, after that hit you took in practice."

"Oh, yeah, that was nothing," I said, gently touching my backside.

"Is Breeze there?"

"Just a moment."

Mute, mute, Breeze was mouthing to me, wanting me to push the button on the phone. I handed over the phone and let her push the button. One of Breeze's golden rules of dating was "Keep them waiting." Unfortunately, since preseason training had begun, Jared was playing that game, too, though maybe not intentionally.

I headed for the bathroom, stopped outside of it to pull a clean towel from the linen closet, and finally heard her say hello in a tone that sounded as if she had no idea who might be on the other end of the phone. "*Oh.* Hi, Jared."

I closed the bathroom door, then remembered her nail polish. Pulling open the drawer on her side of the vanity, I picked up her favorite color, the remover, and an assortment of files, and carried the stuff out to her.

She frowned at the lavender bottle. Or maybe at Jared.

"Excuse me?" she said. "Ex*cuse* me?" she repeated, her voice climbing the scale. "I'm sure I didn't hear you right, Jared."

I went back to get her second and third favorite colors. She grimaced at them—or Jared.

Returning to the bathroom, I removed the entire drawer and carried it to her. I wasn't trying to please her; I was securing alone time in the bathroom.

"What!" she nearly shouted. "What?! Well, chug some Gatorade!" Her face was getting very pink. "It's Friday night, Jared. It's Labor Day weekend!"

First he is screamed at by Coach, then he's screamed at by Breeze. Jared will go deaf, I thought.

"You promised! You promised me! Well, then," she said, her voice dropping in pitch, sounding suddenly calm. If I were him, I'd be getting worried. "I think you had better sit down and reexamine your choices. Perhaps we both need to reconsider our relationship."

She's been watching Dr. Phil again, I thought.

I don't know what Jared said back to Breeze, but she slammed down the phone.

"Jerk!" A fat tear rolled down her face.

I didn't rush over to comfort my sister; I had seen this too many times before.

"What's this for?" she grumbled, looking at the drawer of polish. Her green eyes flicked up at me, bright with anger. "Poor baby," she said sarcastically, "he's tired. He's dehydrated. He needs to stay home and rest."

"Well," I said, standing in her doorway, pulling my sweat-soaked shirt over my head, "Coach was really working them hard today, and it was like a sauna out there."

"I hate Siefert. Hate him."

"The first game is a week from today," I continued.

"Coach is going to work the team really hard for the next several days, then ease up just before the game. That's how it's supposed to be done, at least according to Gabriel."

"Gabriel," she repeated, rolling her eyes, which annoyed me. "Siefert told them to be in bed by nine o'clock. He's going to bed at nine o'clock this whole weekend! What am *I* supposed to do?"

I unzipped my shorts and let them drop. "Can't you get together during the day?"

"You'd think Siefert was Vince Liberti—"

"Lombardi," I corrected.

"—the way Jared obeys! I've had enough of this. Who's he going to listen to, me or Siefert?"

"The thing is, Breeze," I said, as I continued to strip. "Coach will probably have a lot more effect than you on Jared's future." Her eyes flashed and she opened her mouth to answer back, but I went on. "Junior year is a huge year for college recruiting. And he's a star. Jared, Flynn, Mike—they're all good enough to get full scholarships to terrific schools. They're being scouted. They've got to play their best. And Siefert knows how to make them play their best."

"Like *I'm* not part of Jared's future?" she answered back. "Like my love and support won't help him win a scholarship?"

Actually, I believed that true love could be found in

high school. My aunt Sandy fell in love with Uncle Greg during sophomore year, and now they were waiting for their first grandchild. It happens. But to Breeze? In two years, she had gone through at least one player from each sport: football and soccer, basketball and wrestling, lacrosse and—well, none from baseball, but she had made up for that with the lead from our spring musical.

"Jared is going to have to choose," my sister said. "It's me or Siefert."

"I'm not sure I'd offer him that choice."

She turned on me, "Like you know anything about dating! Like you're an expert on guys! You attend dances with your freakin' camera! I mean, maybe for you, it's sweet—"

"I'm taking my shower," I interrupted and turned my back on her. I knew Breeze was just taking out on me her frustration with Jared, but sometimes she said some hurtful things. Because she just bounced along, never taking seriously what someone else said about her, she forgot that other people did.

A half hour later, when I emerged from the steamy bathroom, Breeze apologized.

"I'm sorry, Hayley, I was mad at Jared. When I say stupid things, you should ignore me. You know that. You're my best sister."

"I'm your only sister," I replied, then laughed.

"Want to go to the mall?"

"Tonight? I was going to work on some photos."

"You should always go to sales when the stuff is fresh."

"It depends—"

"No, that's a fact. Once everything is picked over—"

"I mean it depends on whether you are planning to do what you did three weeks ago when we shopped."

"Which is what?" she said, batting her eyes innocently—lined, shadowed, mascara-coated eyes.

"Select my clothes."

"Now, why would I do that?"

"Because we wear the same size?" I suggested.

She smiled a little.

Breeze and I are the exact same shape and size, but most people wouldn't think so. When I'm not crawling on my knees or lying on my stomach to get a good picture, I like dressing soft and pretty. What I don't like is guys looking bug-eyed, staring at me through gaps in tight clothing, any more than I like people noticing the girl behind the camera. It just makes me self-conscious. Breeze has never had a self-conscious moment in her life. To her, it is only natural that everyone, especially guys, can't take their eyes off her.

"I don't borrow from you," my sister said. "For one thing, we can't wear the same colors."

As Breeze has told me again and again, bright red was perfect for a brunette like me. Pastels looked better with her blond coloring, but she longed to wear red, and sometimes did. I wasn't fooled three weeks ago, when she tried to convince me to buy a *very* expensive, clingy, scarlet knit top.

"Come on," she said, "let's grab some dinner and go."

We left a note for Dad, who was working late again. Breeze, who had her provisional license, drove our Mazda—and so did I, since she often waved both hands around when she talked.

The mall was jammed. Supposedly we were looking at the fall clothes which had been put on sale, but two hours into scraping hangers against metal rods, Breeze thrust a bathing suit in my face. "You've *got* to try this on."

"The pool is closing Monday."

"It's on clearance. Look at the price. Do you know how much these suits *usually* go for?"

I took the hanger from her. The bikini was fire engine red. If I developed a sudden cramp, the lifeguard was sure to see me go down.

"Try it," she said. "Please?"

I shrugged. "Why not."

We added it to the pile that we lugged into a shared dressing room. I saved it for last.

"Amazing!" exclaimed Breeze as I modeled it for her. "Absolutely amazing!"

I looked in the mirror. Wow! I'd been filling out in some of the right places.

"What a great cut can do for you!" my sister added. "Let me try it."

I peeled off the suit and handed it over. It fit her just as it fit me, but the color had lost its zing.

"Oh. I guess it's not that great," she said, tossing it aside.

And *that* is when I decided to buy it.

The next morning, I awoke early, saw the bag on my chair, and instantly regretted my purchase. *I'll return it*, I thought, as I rolled over in bed.

But I couldn't—it was a "clearance." I had thrown thirty bucks down the drain, thirty bucks that might have been used for my camera. I told myself that it couldn't really be as red as I remembered. I climbed out of bed and opened the bag. It was. Chlorine would help, but how many laps would I have to swim before the suit stopped signaling bulls?

I glanced at the clock—seven forty-five A.M. Our community pool is opened from eight thirty to nine thirty for lap-swimming only. After that, on the last holiday weekend of the summer, it would be mobbed. *I'll swim with the old people*, I thought, and forced myself to put on my new suit. I pulled a long shirt over it and threw a big towel and some sunblock in a bag. After a bagel and juice, I scribbled a note, leaving it in the usual spot on the kitchen counter, and walked to the pool.

Two saggy middle-aged men, an old woman with a flowered bathing cap, and I all arrived at the same time. The lifeguard climbed into her chair and I pulled off my shirt, dropping it on my towel at the shallow end of the pool, where the other three had deposited their stuff. I took the big clip out of my hair, and shook out the waves.

"Haaay-ley."

I turned around, surprised. "Jared!" I guess it didn't matter what kind of suit I was wearing, Jared's eyes were going to wander. "What are you doing here?" I asked.

"Getting in an easy aerobic workout. I thought it would be just me and the old folks."

"Me too."

"My towel is over there, by the diving board." He pointed.

"I'm probably just going to swim and leave." I put on my goggles like a headband and started walking toward the side of the pool. "Choose your lane," I said to him.

"So how mad *is* Breeze?" he asked.

I shrugged. "I guess that's something you should talk about with her."

"I was hoping you'd tell her how hard Coach is working us and how hot it was on the field yesterday."

Of course, I had, but I wasn't going to admit it, because I didn't like to play the messenger between my sister and her boyfriends. I didn't mind so much when the guys were forced to hang out with me in our family room, while she dressed for their dates. But I resented it when, without warning, she left me to deliver the message that she was out and must have forgotten that they were coming over. And I positively hated it when they hoped I would deliver messages to her.

"Maybe you could kind of keep her company for me," Jared suggested, "while Coach is hot on our backs."

Like I had nothing better to do than be a companion to my sister?

"I don't think so." My tone was way sharp, and I saw his eyes widen a little. "Listen, Jared, why don't you try to explain to her, you know, really spell it out, what Coach is asking of you, which scouts will be in the stands, what kind of competition you are up against from other players who want the same scholarships, that kind of thing."

"See," he said, "*you* understand."

"And you have to give Breeze a chance to understand, by explaining it."

"I thought maybe you could help and—"

I shook my head. "Sorry. It's got to come from you." *Besides*, I thought, *she's already made it clear she won't listen to me.*

I chose the lane between the flowered bathing cap and the saggy bald guy, so that Jared and I wouldn't be discussing his girlfriend problems between laps.

The water felt great and I swam and swam. When I finally pulled myself out, only the flowered cap and Jared were still going. I laid down on my towel to dry. With the sun warming my back, I quickly fell asleep and began to dream. I was at football practice. Gray eyes, eyes that could turn mystical blue, were looking at me over the black grid of a face mask. Flynn was smiling and for a single moment I thought I might—

Then I heard my sister's voice. "This is a surprise!"

I rolled over sleepily. "Didn't you see my note on the counter?"

"Hi, Breeze."

I jumped at the sound of a voice so close to my ear. I was lying arm against arm with Jared!

"What are you doing here?" I asked, sitting up quickly, looking toward the diving board area, where he had supposedly left his things. Now his striped beach towel was wedged in between mine and the chair of the bald swimmer.

Jared laughed. "Why do you keep asking me that?"

"Doesn't look like there's much room for me," Breeze remarked.

"There's plenty," I said, shifting to my knees, throwing my sunblock and goggles in my bag. "I was just drying off and fell asleep." I pulled my T-shirt over my head and picked up my towel. "I've got folders of pictures to work on at home. See you guys."

"Got any great pictures of me?" Jared called. "Got any copies I could have?"

I was eager to get out of there. Fortunately, an army of noisy kids had arrived. I turned back, tugged my earlobe, and shook my head, pretending I couldn't hear him.

Then I heard him say to Breeze. "Your sister looks really hot in that suit."

I wished someone other than Jared had said it; still, enjoying the protection of my long shirt, I found myself walking a little sassier.

Of course, his compliment wasn't the best strategy for encouraging Breeze to forgive a nine o'clock curfew. *Was Jared that dumb*, I wondered, *or simply insensitive?* Or was there, by any chance, a few active brain cells in that large piece of sirloin, plotting to make her jealous, hoping she would then be grateful for whatever time he could give her?

Who knew?

Who cared!

3

The Courier came out Friday, the end of our first week of school. Sometimes it seemed like a miracle when the stories and pictures finally came together, and this was one of those times. Our editor in chief, Kathleen, was great, but our assistant editor, Dillon, was a pain—more interested in making a splash than covering the news accurately.

I had been so busy Tuesday, Wednesday, and Thursday getting used to classes and working on photographs, I hadn't noticed much about Breeze and Jared, except that they were having a lot of phone fights. Friday evening, I slipped on my khakis with all the great pockets, while

Breeze tugged on jeans that had been made from a wax cast of her body (only kidding), and we headed for the game. I needed to get there early so I could load up my cameras and fill my pockets with extra batteries, memory sticks, and a small notepad for jotting down names of any nonplayers I photographed.

Gabriel caught up with me inside the stadium. "Why is your sister painting her nails in the newspaper office?"

"Not by the computers, right? I told her to stay clear of them. But she was nice enough to rush her schedule and drive me here, and she has to get fixed up somewhere."

One of our feature writers, Paige, came up behind me. "Breeze is in the office? Maybe I can get a pregame interview."

Gabriel rolled his eyes. "An interview asking her *what*? If Flynn is this year's go-to man for Jared? How often Jared's going to throw into the flat? Are Flynn and Jared going to be the best TD combo in our school's history? She knows nothing about football!"

Paige laughed. "You just don't get it, Gabe. Football is only a small part of tonight. Look at the crowd."

Twenty minutes before the game, people were already pouring in. Football was very big at our school, and it wasn't just the students who showed up. All of Saylor Mill loved "Friday Nights Under the Lights."

As for Paige, I had a certain respect for her skills, which was something Gabriel couldn't understand. I admired the fact that she had a signature look: chestnut-colored hair, cut in a sleek chin-length bob, and bright red lipstick. Raised by her grandparents, I think she may have watched too many girl-reporter movies from way back when, but somehow, for her, the look worked. And the bottom line was that she could sniff out information like you wouldn't believe, and she could write, I mean, she could churn it out. When she wasn't working on the newspaper, she was posting long chapters of her romance on an Internet fiction site.

Tonight, Paige carried, as usual, a red notebook and a mini tape recorder, along with a small point-and-shoot digital.

"Are the rumors true?" she asked me. "Are Breeze and Jared fighting like pit bulls?"

"Don't know."

"Nicole said they're on the road to breakup."

I slipped a film cartridge into the school's oldest, crankiest camera, which still turned out excellent prints.

"Of course, Nicole has always had it out for Breeze, and Breeze doesn't like Nicole, even though they often pretend to get along as football widows."

"Football widows!" Gabriel exclaimed. "They're not

married, so how can they—"

Paige continued, "Everyone knows that Breeze's eyes wander if the guy she's dating doesn't keep *his* eye on her."

I shrugged.

"Who are they wandering to?" Paige asked.

I could have told her that Breeze's eyes were pretty much always on the roam.

"Can you take a guess?" Paige persisted.

"How many more questions before you give up?" I asked.

Paige laughed. "One of these days, Hayley, I'm going to suck a piece of gossip out of you. Well, I'm off."

After she was out of earshot, Gabriel turned to me. "*Are* they fighting?"

"Gabriel Milano!" I exclaimed. "Isn't that question beneath you as a reporter solely interested in sports and international news?"

"I have other interests. I just don't talk about them much."

"Really," I said, smiling. "Well, the cheerleaders have finished their stretches. I need to get some pom-pom shots."

I got those photos, along with a few shots of cute little kids jumping around at the refreshment booth, the usual hammy pictures of fans in the stands, then a series of the players running into the stadium through an archway of balloons. I waited for the one I really wanted, the players standing along the sideline, red helmets held by their sides, hands over their hearts, during the national anthem. The expressions on their faces, the sense of excitement and anticipation hanging in the air, and that feeling of time suspended were perfect for a still shot.

Flynn was on my end of the long line of players. His eyes were raised to the flag and his thick, dark hair ruffled in the breeze. He was one of the lucky guys whose cheeks actually showed it when he decided not to shave that day—very rough, very heart-stopping for the girls who got close, if not for the other team. It was so tempting to use my telephoto. But I was a disciplined journalist, and though whim-of-the-moment shots often turned out well, I first had to cover the "assignments" I had set for myself. Besides, when reviewing my photos from the previous year, I noticed I had zoomed in on Flynn like thirty times too many. Even when I was covering dances, I had a lot of pictures of him, although I blamed that on his girlfriend, Nicole, who was a real camera flirt. As for me, it wasn't like I was in love with him or something—I've never even spoken to him, except to say "Hold it right there" or "Cheese." No, I had nothing more dangerous than what I call a "camera crush."

The game began and I moved up and down the sidelines, clicking away. The first quarter, while the team was establishing their running game, I didn't get anything worth printing. Piled up bodies make for lousy photos. But second quarter, Jared began some serious passing. By the time we were on the twenty yard line, I had two terrific shots of Jared rearing back and firing, and three of our receivers in midair. Flynn, who was six foot four, was spectacular at getting up high for the ball. He snatched a pass that seemed to carry him into the stadium lights. The crowd went wild.

We were first-and-goal. And if there is anyone in the stadium who gets as stressed as Coach Siefert when we are first-and-goal, it's me, wondering how I am going to get *the* shot of the touchdown. The opposing team called a time-out. Gabriel came to stand next to me, just outside the end zone.

"Who's taking it in for them?" I asked.

"Well," Gabriel began, "there are a number of possibilities."

"I don't want possibilities. I want the name of the player I should be focusing on."

"How many times do I have to explain to you, Hayley, that even if I knew the play, the guy could be covered and—"

"You don't have to explain. I'm just being nervous. I

wish I could clone myself."

"You could allow someone else to use a camera," he said slyly.

"You know Siefert's rules, only one student photographer on the sidelines."

"What I know is that you follow the rules *you* like, and find ways around the other ones." The teams were lining up along the six yard line. "I'd say, for the first down, they're going to run it. To the left."

When the team did, I turned to Gabriel. "Nice call."

"Did you see how open Mark was in the corner of the end zone? I'm sure Siefert did."

I took that as a hint and mentally prepared myself to shoot the corner. But the snap was fumbled and we barely recovered it, so I had another nice photo of jumbled up arms and legs.

"Flynn," said Gabriel. "I'd go to Flynn. It's third down. He's the one Jared has the most confidence in."

"Won't the other team know that?"

"With Flynn, it doesn't matter," Gabriel replied. "He thrives under pressure. He can make it happen."

I watched through my viewfinder as Jared barked out the play, took the snap, and dropped back three steps. Everybody was on the move. Jared scrambled away from one tackle, reset, pumped once, pumped twice. . . . And then I saw it unfolding, as if in slow motion. Flynn was gliding across the end zone. Defenders moved toward him, one from either side. The football flew like a perfectly targeted missile to a height that only Flynn could reach. My eyes were quicker than my brain and felt wired directly to my fingers. Three players and a ball coming together. "Great shot, great shot, great shot!" my brain was screaming as Flynn's hands encircled the ball.

Then I heard the awful crunch of equipment and a sickening thud, one which reminded me that there were heavy bodies out there, going full speed and hurling themselves against the flimsy protection of pads. The three players went down in a heap. Two of them got up. Flynn did not. I felt my stomach contract. The wild cheers of the crowd fell silent.

One of the players quickly knelt by Flynn. The other shouted and waved frantically at the sideline. Siefert and his coaches came out at a dead run and pushed aside Flynn's gathering teammates.

Gabriel's voice came in a whisper. "He isn't moving. Hayley, he isn't moving."

"Oh, God."

Gabriel and I stood so close to each other, our upper arms were pressed together. A man and woman with medical bags followed the coaches onto the field. The players formed circles and held hands in a show of team support.

"Please remain in your seats. For the safety of all, please remain in your seats," the voice on the PA system said. Some of the students from the stands, friends of Flynn, were trying to get onto the field. I saw the teachers who had come to the game forming a makeshift barrier at the edge of the stands.

"This is bad," Gabriel said.

"Could be bad, you mean *could be*, right?"

"Shouldn't you be covering this?" he asked.

I glanced down at the camera in my hand. I didn't want to. But what kind of photojournalist was I, if I couldn't shoot an injured football player? What kind of professional could I be if I let personal feelings—not that I had any real personal feelings for him—get in my way. "I guess."

"You could just do crowd pictures," Gabriel suggested. "And if everything works out okay, we can caption them something like, 'a scary moment at the game' and let the crowd picture tell the story."

"Right." I heard the wail of a siren in the distance.

I turned to look for my sister, knowing that the cool crowd, including players' girlfriends, always sat at the fifty yard line, one-third the way up the stands. I saw Breeze shift her position and tilt her head for a moment, and I knew she was looking back at me. Sometimes it was like telepathy—no message, just a kind of link. Feeling better, I began to take photos of the crowd and the other players. The paramedics arrived. I saw Nicole, Flynn's girlfriend, fighting her way through the people on the field. She turned and met my camera's eye.

A few minutes later a gurney with a stiff board on top was rolled to the end zone.

"Can you see anything?" I asked Gabriel, debating whether to seek a higher position in the stands.

"No. I guess they are loading him on. They've got to be careful, in case there is damage to the spine or neck."

"Like the kind—the kind that ends up in paralysis?" I said, my voice trailing off.

It seemed to take forever. Then, suddenly, there was a gap in the crowd as people pulled back, allowing the paramedics to wheel the gurney across the grass.

Flynn, lying on his back, raised his head slightly, as if trying to see around him.

"He's moving!" Gabriel said with relief.

Flynn lifted his left forearm to give a thumbs-up sign. The crowd cheered.

A moment later I realized I wasn't looking at the scene through a camera. It was Nicole who made me realize it.

There is some kind of homing device in Nicole that always finds me and the camera, and now she was holding on to the rolling gurney rather melodramatically, looked over at me expectantly. I quickly lifted the digital. Fortunately, Flynn, responding to the cheers from the crowd, gave them a second thumbs-up. Nicole gazed down at him with an expression of grief and hope that was badly over-acted, if you ask me, but I was there as a journalist, not a movie director. *Click, click, click.*

After the ambulance took him away, the teams began to play again, but halfheartedly. Then someone shouted, "For Flynn! For Flynn!" and the action heated up.

It was late in the fourth quarter, our team was ahead by what turned out to be the game-winning field goal, when the PA announcer told us that Flynn had suffered a mild concussion and broken his arm. We were asked to check the school website for information over the weekend, and not to bother his family.

Gabriel shook his head. "There goes our season."

4

Flynn's injury quieted the arguments between Breeze and Jared—temporarily. But by Monday night, after Coach's rousing call to everyone to step up their game, the two of them were back at it.

Tuesday morning, as Breeze turned into the school parking lot, it was obvious that my sister's attention to everyday tasks, like driving, was wandering. Our Mazda wandered over to the left lane, which didn't make the driver who was coming from the opposite direction too happy. Thanks to that driver's blasting horn, Breeze caught the attention of Flynn, whom she pulled up next to. Jared, who was just getting out of his little red car, also noticed us.

"Hey, Flynn," my sister said.

From the passenger side, all I could see was Flynn's right arm in a cast and sling, and his left forearm and huge hand holding a stack of books against his ribs.

"Hi, Breeze. How's it going?"

"How's it going for *you*?" she cooed.

"Not bad," he said cheerfully.

Of course, that was the moment I should have leaned across the car so that Flynn could see me through the window and should've said kind of casually, "Hey, hope you're doing okay." But I remained invisible, staring at the swollen, purple fingers of his right hand. Maybe it was being just a few feet away with no camera between us, but Flynn seemed too . . . too real. Unable to see his face and incredible eyes, I became acutely aware of his voice.

"One thing I've learned," Flynn told Breeze, "is not to take my right arm for granted. My mother had to cut my meat last night!"

She laughed. "Since you can't write, are they going to excuse you from tests and papers?"

"No, they're going to give me extra time to peck on a keyboard."

"Well, I'm sure there are a lot of kids who will be happy to help you," she said, turning her head slightly, her eyes sliding to the right to see if Jared was coming toward us. I knew how my sister operated; she was counting on it.

"Hey, Jared," Flynn greeted him.

Jared's stomach and arms joined Flynn's at the driver-side window. Meanwhile, of course, I was getting all kinds of dirty looks from people who were forced to drive on the wrong side of the road—my side—to get around our car. No one honked, perhaps out of respect for Flynn.

"What's up, Breeze?" Jared asked. I could hear the tension in his voice.

"I was telling Flynn, with him being one-armed and all, I'm glad to help him out. We have all the same lunches. And I *certainly* have time on my hands in the afternoon and evening."

Jab, I thought.

"He's still part of the team," Jared replied coolly, "and Coach is encouraging us to eat together as a team."

She laughed and shrugged her shoulders. "Well, then, I'll just be a good friend in the afternoon and evening."

Jab, jab.

"I'll be around, Flynn."

"That's nice of you," he said. "Uh, I think we're causing a traffic jam here."

My sister calmly surveyed the line-up of cars that were trying to squeeze through the one lane she had left open for drivers coming from two directions. The color was high in her cheeks and her green eyes had a danger-ous shine in them.

"I don't believe in slavishly following rules," she replied, "not Siefert's, not anybody's." Then she pulled directly into the open lane with no warning to the other drivers. Horns blasted. Breeze threw back her head and laughed. I closed my eyes till we were safely docked in a space.

Wednesday morning, after another hair-raising adventure with Breeze in the school parking lot, I went to the news-paper office. Things were buzzing the way they always do the day we go to press. Several people were working on the computers at one end of the rectangular room. Our editor in chief, Kathleen, was studying copy at the confer-ence table in the middle. Dillon, the assistant editor, was sitting in one of the several comfortable chairs grouped at the other end of the long room, his feet up, looking like he thought his last name was Hearst.

I loved the *Courier* office—loved it when we were gathered around the conference table, bouncing ideas off one another, loved it on mornings like this when sunlight was streaming through its three sets of long windows and keys were clicking away.

"News flash!" Paige announced, as she entered the room. "Stop the presses!"

Like I said before, she's seen too many old girl-reporter movies. People typed on. Dillon rose and joined Kathleen at the conference table.

"But I really *do* have big news! Nicole has dumped Flynn."

The typing stopped. Even Gabriel, who was on a PC in the far corner, looked up.

"Flynn Delancy?" somebody asked.

"No way!" said somebody else.

Paige gave the juicy details. The killing blow was delivered by handwritten letter, or e-mail, or, according to one of her sources, in person at Papa John's. Whatever. One person said Nicole cried crocodile tears, saying that she feared she was hurting Flynn deeply. Another source said she laughed in his face. A third claimed that he stormed out of Papa John's and knocked a pile of napkins to the floor. Whatever. But the amazing truth, which all sources confirmed, was that *she* was the one who ended the long, steady relationship. Flynn got dumped!

"Well," I said, as everyone talked about this shocking bit of gossip instead of working on the paper, which was due to the printer at four P.M., "maybe we should put out one of those *People* magazine special editions, devoted totally to Flynn Delancy—his athletic career, his injury, and his love life." I saw the bright flicker in Paige's eyes.

41

"I'm kidding, Paige, just kidding!"

Dillon flexed his hands, then folded them on the table in front of him. "So, how are we going to handle the photo?"

"Which photo?" Gabriel asked.

"*The* photo," Kathleen replied. She ran her fingers through her short brown hair. "The one with Flynn giving the inspiring thumbs-up."

"And with Nicole at his gurney's side," Dillon added, "looking like a cross between Mother Teresa and Angelina Jolie."

We burst out laughing.

"Can't you delete her?" Jenny asked me. Jenny covered arts and entertainment for the paper, mostly movies, and was working at the computer next to Gabriel.

"You mean send Nicole to Photoshop heaven?" I replied. "I can, but I won't."

"Not enough time?" asked Dillon.

I flashed him a look. "On *principle*!"

"What principle is that?" asked Paige.

"This is a newspaper, not a pop culture magazine. We're journalists. Nicole was there. She was mugging for the camera. And if you use the picture, she is going to stay there. I *won't* misrepresent what happened."

"But what about Flynn's feelings?" Jenny asked. "It

would be so totally embarrassing for him."

"He's a jock," I said, "and jocks have egos the size of Saturn. He'll survive it."

"Any input, Gabe?" Kathleen asked. "You're the sports editor."

"I agree with Hayley. I don't think we should doctor photos that way. Adjusting lighting is one thing, changing a fact is another. And besides," he added, "from the behavior of the girls I've seen in the hall, I'd say Flynn isn't going to suffer from embarrassment for too long."

"Really? Names, names," Paige prompted.

Gabriel ignored her.

"Well, the real photo will be fantastic for circulation," Dillon pointed out. "We won't have any papers left over. I vote for principle—*this* time."

"So," said Kathleen, turning to me, "you're saying we go with the photo as is, or not at all."

"A good newspaper tells it like it is," I replied. "And if a photo shows that a girl is a conniving fake and a guy is an idiot for getting sucked in, too bad, that's the way it is."

"On the other hand," said Kathleen, with a calmness that had won her the top job, "we are a school newspaper, not *The New York Times*. I don't see why we should embarrass someone who has contributed a lot to our school with a picture that comments on gossip rather than news. Can you find another good photo for that spot before four o'clock?" she asked me.

I sighed. "Sure. But for the record, *I* would work the same way, whether I'm covering for *The New York Times* or *The Courier*."

"Noted," Kathleen replied with a smile. "And thanks, Hayley."

5

After putting the newspaper to bed, several of us hung around the office. Paige read to us the latest chapter of her romance (and Gabriel made a quick exit), then Kathleen, Jenny, and I posted complimentary reviews on her fiction site. At five o'clock it was just Jenny and me, talking movies. Her mother teaches film courses, and Jenny notices things about movies I'd never think to look for. It's cool.

When I finally got home, I was surprised to find my dad in the kitchen, lifting the lid of a pot, as if he didn't know a pile of limp noodles lay inside.

It was 6:18 and Mrs. Klein had her purse and vinyl

shopping bag in hand.

"Hi, Mrs. Klein. Hey, Dad. Project over?"

"Hi, honey. For now," he said. "It's great to see you."

I dropped my backpack at my feet, though I knew it would merit what Breeze and I called "one eyebrow" from Mrs. Klein as she passed by.

"I'll get out another plate," I said, seeing there were just two on the kitchen island.

"Breeze says she has no appetite," Mrs. Klein said.

I glanced from her to my father. "Is something wrong?"

"Nothing *new*," Mrs. Klein replied. "Good night, Mr. Caldwell. Good night, Hayley."

"G'night." I turned to Dad as the door closed behind her.

"I think it's boy trouble," he said.

My father, who works for NASA and helps design machines that will be launched into space a decade or so from now, lives the rest of his life in the previous century, and uses terms like "boy trouble."

"Did Breeze and Jared have another fight?"

"A big one, it appears. She won't come out of her room. I was going to make her a nice warm plate of buttered noodles."

I smiled. Dad's response to any crisis that he considered beyond his ability to discuss (and nowadays, most of them were) was buttered something—noodles, toast, popcorn.

"Why don't I check on her and see what's going on," I said. "Are you starved?" He was tall and lean, and always looked hungry to me.

"I can wait," he replied, padding off in his socks to his favorite chair in the family room.

I carried my backpack to my room, washed my face, then knocked softly on Breeze's door.

"Go away."

"It's me."

A moment later the door opened. Breeze's face looked pink and puffy.

"Hi."

"Hi."

"So, I guess today's entry in your diary isn't going to start with, '*Everything is fab*,'" I said.

"Nope."

"Want to talk about it?"

She thought for a moment, then stepped aside to let me in. At first I couldn't tell if she was going through another wardrobe planning session, or she had been throwing things in a tantrum. Then I saw the long spiky heel of her favorite purple shoes impaled in one of Jared's posed "quarterback" photos that I had given her.

She saw me staring at it. "We broke up."

After all the fights, I shouldn't have been surprised, but this was just the beginning of the season, and with Flynn out, Jared would be *the* hero.

"I'm sorry, Breeze. I really am."

"Well, I guess somebody should be."

"You're not?" I asked, looking into her red eyes.

She walked away from me and stopped at her bureau to pick up her brush. She began to brush her hair, each stroke harder than the previous.

"Please be careful," I said. "I'm very attached to that beautiful golden hair."

She paused, her mouth quivering.

"I really am sorry, Breeze. I wish I knew how to make you feel better."

"Jared said that with all the pressure that was on him right now, he knew he couldn't give me the attention I deserved. He said it wasn't fair to me. I should be free to date whoever I want."

"*Really*," I said, surprised. "That was kind of decent of him."

"Decent!" she exclaimed.

"Well . . . thoughtful."

"Thoughtful!" she screamed. "You are *so* naïve, Hayley. You know nothing about dating guys."

"Breeze, since football camp began, you've been fighting and saying—"

"I am perfectly capable of deciding on my own to date whoever I want," Breeze interrupted me. "I don't need *him* to give me permission. Who does he think he is!"

"Your boyfriend?" I suggested.

"I am perfectly able to find the attention I deserve—and more! Guys are always hitting on me. I certainly don't need a push from him in that direction."

"I see."

"Hayley, he wasn't being thoughtful. He was being a coward. He was breaking up and pretending it was the best thing for me."

I thought about the situation. "So, what if it is the best thing for you?"

She stared at me, wanting sympathy rather than a rational response. "You just don't understand these things."

Maybe, but I did understand why she wasn't answering my question. If she admitted it might be the best thing for her, then she wouldn't be able to rant and rave and ask for sympathy. But if she admitted that this was not a good thing, she would be putting herself in the role of "dumped." As far back as I could remember, Breeze had never been dumped.

"Come have dinner with Dad and me."

"I'm not hungry."

"We'd just like to have you around," I said. "I don't know why, but we miss you when you're not there." I gave her a quick hug, then left, and finally heard her footsteps following behind.

School was buzzing Thursday and Friday, and Paige spun down the locker-lined halls, through the cafeteria, and in and out of the newspaper office like a red tornado. Flynn and Nicole. Breeze and Jared. Who would have guessed?

Perhaps I should have felt worse for Flynn and Breeze, both of them finding themselves unexpectedly dumped. But I had been through so many breakups with Breeze— and listened to her brokenhearted boyfriends, who, after all that time hanging out in our family room, mistook me for their sister—I just couldn't get all worked up about it. Besides, the cool and the gorgeous usually survive. And there were a million girls feeling sympathetic toward Flynn. I exaggerate, there were only six to eight at any one time clustered around him.

"What *was* Nicole thinking?" Paige asked, shaking her head.

Of course, it was terribly tacky to dump a guy four days after a season-ending injury, an injury over which an entire stadium had held its breath. But I knew how Nicole's mind worked.

She ran in the same ultracool circles that Breeze did, and it was important for her that she not only liked the guy she dated, but that he gave her status. He was expected to provide a ticket to events that were cool to be seen at. She was smart enough to know that, while Flynn was hero of the moment, with each new football game, his rating would drop, at least as compared to the cool ratings of other players. In a sense, both Coach Siefert and she were scanning the team to see who would replace Flynn. Unlike Coach, she had other leagues to consider. Word flew fast that she had attended the drama group tryouts Thursday afternoon. *Perhaps*, I thought, *she was as sick of the football schedule as Breeze.*

Friday's football game was at a school about twenty minutes away from Saylor Mill. Kids traveled in caravans, and Gabriel, Jenny, and I hitched a ride with Kathleen.

Unfortunately for Kathleen, she was fast becoming "den mother." Her boyfriend was in his first year at a Pennsylvania college and wasn't interested in coming home. So she spent her time on the newspaper, several tough AP courses, and us—driving us around.

Breeze asked if she could come with us that night. We squeezed together and let her sit quietly, staring out the window. Since my sister could have driven herself, I figured she was really hurting. Knowing the coaches of other teams were not as fanatical about rules as Siefert, I made an offer. "Would you like to hang with me on the sidelines?" I asked. "I've got an extra camera you can wear around your neck."

For a moment her eyes went misty. "You're my best sister!"

"Your only," I reminded her.

She nodded. "But I'm cool. I can deal with this. I guess I'll find out who my real friends are," she added, and headed for the stands in an outfit that would draw guys like flies to honey. Oh, yeah, she could deal with this.

In the course of the game, it looked as if a junior named Gavin Thompson might replace Flynn, especially after he snagged a pass, shook off two defenders, and ran in for a touchdown. Too bad he fumbled on the next offensive effort, and the other team recovered it and ran it in for a score. Really too bad, because we lost to a team we should have beaten.

After the fumble, Flynn went over and stood next to Gavin—didn't say anything, just stood next to him. It was the only way one player could support another who'd made a terrible mistake: just be there for him and say through your actions, *that's okay, we're in this together*. I found myself admiring Flynn for doing that, especially when nobody else did.

As agreed earlier, those of us who came with Kathleen gathered at her car fifteen minutes after the game ended. Breeze sent a message through Jenny that she had found another ride home. Kathleen made the rounds, dropping us off at our front doors, and I was the last one.

Entering our house, standing in the entrance to the family room, I could see that a light was on in the kitchen. I knew Dad went to bed early after long projects like his last. "Hi, Breeze," I called in to my sister.

"Hey, Hayley," she called back.

"That game sure was the pits," I said, setting down my camera bag and pack. "We could have done better if Flynn had played one-armed, and if he'd left his head and helmet on the bench!"

Breeze didn't reply, but a round of deep laughter came from the kitchen. Her ride home.

"I guess you're hungry," Breeze called out to me.

"Have I ever come back from watching beefy guys beat each other up and not wanted something from the deli drawer?"

Another deep laugh.

Breeze knew I liked to eat after games. I figured that if she had wanted privacy, she would have taken her "ride home" to the back deck.

"I have a zillion pictures to download," I said, entering the kitchen. "I'm just going to make a sandwich to—to, uh, take, uh . . . to my room."

"Hello." Flynn's voice was as warm as his smile. He and Breeze were sitting on the barstools along one side of our center island. His slate-colored eyes gazed at me with friendly curiosity.

"Hi."

"This is my sister, Hayley," Breeze said.

"Really? I wouldn't have guessed." He looked from me to Breeze. "I don't think I even knew you had a sister."

"We're twins," I told him.

He glanced at me with surprise. I shouldn't have said it, but he wasn't the first guy who found it amazing that Breeze and I came from the same gene pool.

"Uh, fraternal," he replied, uncertainly, and Breeze laughed. She was using her girly, tinkling laugh.

"Just kidding," I told him, and turned my back, glad to have a refrigerator to open and stare into. *Why did she have to choose him?* I thought. Of course, both of them had just been jilted, so it was natural enough that they'd find each other. Had she flirted first? Maybe he had. Why should I care?

"Hayley is a sophomore," Breeze told Flynn.

54

"Do you go to Saylor Mill?" he asked.

I turned toward him holding a bag of meat and the mayo jar, with perhaps not the friendliest look on my face. Apparently he had never noticed me on the sidelines. I wondered if he would have recognized Gabriel. *He'd have to*, I thought, *Gabriel did interviews*. And then again, if your ego is the size of Saturn . . .

"I guess so," he said, "if you just came from the game."

I took out a plate and an evil-looking knife (we'd forgotten to turn the dishwasher on, so our everyday silverware was dirty). Breeze, equally unwilling to hand wash something, had gotten two good china bowls out of the dining room corner cupboard.

"Chocolate swirl or butter pecan?" she asked Flynn, as she slipped off her stool and opened the freezer.

"Whatever is open," he said, then turned to me. "Saylor is a huge school."

"Yes, it is."

"And, of course, the way the class schedules are, people from different years don't cross over in the hallway that much."

"If ever," I said, not because I wanted to get him off the hook, but because I wanted to end a miserable conversation that proved he had never even *slightly* noticed me, despite the fact that I was the only one who photographed the team.

"Hayley does all the photo coverage for the football team," Breeze told him.

"She does?"

I glanced up from the meat I was piling onto my slab of bread.

"You do?" At least he was polite enough to turn pink.

I wiped my hands on a dish towel, picked up my own digital, which I had left on the kitchen counter, and held it up in front of my face. "Now do I look familiar?"

His color deepened.

"Don't worry about it," I said, setting down the camera. "At practice, Coach is always telling you to focus. He'd be thrilled to know how well you're listening."

Flynn looked at me long and thoughtfully, and now I could feel myself turning pink. I flattened my roast beef with a second piece of bread and sliced the sandwich with one stroke of the evil-looking knife.

"About two weeks ago," Flynn said, "I ran over a photographer on the sidelines."

"You didn't tell me that!" Breeze exclaimed to me. Then she added, "*That's* where you got that big bruise on your butt. It was amazing, Flynn, all different shades of purple, like a bouquet of pansies."

"Thank you for that detail, Breeze," I said, and turned

to put away the meat and mayo. I couldn't wait to get out of there.

But as I picked up my sandwich, Flynn ducked his head, trying to catch my eye, trying to make me look at him. It was impossible to look away. Maybe that was how he beat his opponents—he hypnotized them with his gorgeous eyes.

"I hope you're okay," he said.

"Yes, I have some natural padding there."

He held on to my eyes. "I, uh, I'm really sorry."

I knew from his tone he was apologizing not only for tossing me on my rump, but for never noticing me. Now my ego was bruised more than my butt had ever been.

"Not a problem," I told him, and got out of the kitchen as fast as I could.

Five minutes later, I was staring at photos on my computer screen and sipping the flat Coke I had found in my room—I'd been in too big a hurry to remember to grab a drink. I couldn't figure out why it bothered me so much that Flynn Delancy was in our kitchen. Maybe it was because his presence there broke the sacred rules of a camera crush.

A camera crush isn't much different from any kind of secret crush. Lots of people have had the experience of that one face that captures your attention from across a crowded room—in my case, it was across a crowded football field and on the other side of a telephoto lens. Whatever. The rules of having a secret crush were that you tingled a little when you saw that face, you imagined things about the person who belonged to the face—things that probably had nothing to do with who the person really was—and you never, *ever* crossed the distance between you and that person. It would ruin the dream! It would blow away the fantasy!

Unfortunately, when a secret crush begins eating stuff out of your refrigerator, he becomes a little too real.

I had just finished my flat soda when Breeze knocked on my door.

"Come in."

She stood for several minutes, watching over my shoulder as I clicked on the four game photos that I thought were my best.

"You're really good at what you do, Hayley."

"Thanks. This new camera the school bought really helps. It writes incredibly fast to the disk."

"Mmm," she said, already losing interest. Then she laughed and threw herself across my bed. "What *was* I thinking? What *was* I ever thinking?"

I clicked on another photo and rotated it on my screen. "You have to make it easier for me to guess. What were you thinking *when*?"

"When I dated Jared."

"Oh." I sighed. "Probably the same thing you thought when you dated all the other guys."

"But this time things are different," Breeze said. "He's gorgeous, isn't he?"

"Who?" I asked. Like I didn't know!

"Flynn. Flynn Delancy."

"Yeah, he's gorgeous."

She pulled herself up on her elbow. "He's not like any guy I've dated."

I'd heard those words before.

"He's got a great body. Eyes to die for. A sense of humor."

"A high rating in the School of Cool," I added.

"All in one package," Breeze said, leaping up from the bed and spinning around. I had to laugh. If this had been a musical, she would have broken into song.

"Did you ask him for a ride?"

"No," Breeze replied. "No no no! Flynn asked me. He found me during halftime, actually came looking for me! It's nice to be *appreciated*."

She looked over my shoulder again. "Those are photos from tonight's game," she said, sounding disappointed.

"Well, yeah."

"Do you have some from other games on this computer?"

"Sure."

"Print me out some pictures of Flynn," she said, leaning down to give me a hug from behind. "You're my best sister!"

She danced out the door, and I continued to work on the photos I had just taken, though not as happily as before.

6

ate Sunday morning, Dad listened to my proposal, gazing at me over the top of his reading glasses. His hair was mussed up, his glasses perched crookedly on his nose, and three different Sunday papers were spread out before him on the dining room table. That's my dad, a cute nerd. "Well, Hayley, with this heat, the grass won't grow much, and Fred said he'll be back next weekend, but if you really want to cut it . . ."

"I do."

"Still saving for that camera?"

"Yeah."

He smiled and returned to his reading.

"Nice outfit!" Breeze said to me, as she entered the room, tying up the straps of her bikini and smelling of baby oil.

I plucked at my cotton tank top, which once—last year—had two little buttons at the bottom of its scooped neck. The fabric was missing a few threads as well, and my shorts were looking shabby, but cotton soaked up sweat, and thin cotton "breathed." Besides, it was only going to be me and Breeze in the backyard. "It's hot out there."

"Tell me about it," she said, sorting through the papers to pull out the comics. "My plan for school clothes is absolutely ruined. But at least I can maintain my tan."

"Take water with you," my father told us, as we headed outside.

I left a box of lawn bags and a water bottle on the small deck table next to the lounge chair where Breeze stretched out. After unlocking the shed door, I dragged out our cranky mower, filled it with gasoline, and started. The mower was loud and smelly. Pushing it back and forth across the yard, with the sun beating down on me, I zoned out from everything around me.

Halfway through the lawn, I paused to empty the grass catcher and heard Breeze's favorite CD. She had stopped using headphones, so I figured she was on her cell. As I transferred grass clippings from the canvas bag to the plastic, I heard her laugh, then I heard Flynn laugh, and I spilled grass all over. I quickly crouched with my back toward them and picked up clumps of the loose green stuff. Pieces of it stuck to my sweaty arms and legs. *Great*, I thought, *I look like I'm growing green fur*.

Wanting water and needing bags, I glanced over my shoulder, debating what to do. Flynn sprawled in the lounge next to Breeze's. I studied the six-foot privacy hedge that surrounded our yard, longing for a machete. *Well, Flynn wouldn't be the first of Breeze's guys to see me at my worst*, I told myself, as I walked toward the deck.

Flynn and Breeze turned toward me at the same time.

"I need bags. And water."

"Hi, Hayley," Flynn said, smiling.

"Hi."

His eyes followed the sweaty, grassy trail from my neck to my feet. "Looks like you're working hard."

"Yup."

Now his eyes flicked up to the top of my head. Self-consciously, I reached into my mess of tied-up hair and discovered a maple twig. His smiled widened as I removed the leafy branch.

"Why don't you take a break, and I'll pick up where you left off," he offered.

Breeze raised her plucked eyebrows. "One armed?"

He laughed. "I think I can handle it."

"Thanks, but I'm doing it to earn money," I told him. I had to reach between the two of them to get my bottle from the small deck table.

"She's saving for some kind of fancy camera," Breeze explained, as I took a long drink.

"Yeah? What kind?"

"An Olympus, a film camera with fabulous lenses."

"So you like film better than digital?" he asked.

I took another sip. "I have a decent digital. But I really need to understand film. Each medium has its own strength, and I want to learn both."

He nodded as if he understood, as if he were actually interested.

"I want to try black and white, and do it the old-fashioned way, developing it myself, working with an enlarger. I think it's important to understand the history of photography—what I mean is, to experience the history by doing it, to understand better the layers of process that come together when making a photograph and, well, that's all," I concluded, realizing I had warmed too much to my topic—and my listener. "I need ice."

"I'll get it," he offered.

"Thanks, I can do it myself."

"I was just getting some more for Breeze and me."

"So you already know your way around." As soon as I

said it, I wanted to bite my tongue.

One side of his mouth pulled up. "Refrigerators are kind of easy to pick out."

Breeze took my bottle and placed it in Flynn's left hand. His fingers were long enough to grasp easily the three plastic containers. After he had disappeared through the French doors, I borrowed Breeze's small hand towel to dry my face. "Did you know he was coming over?"

Breeze smiled and lifted her beautiful golden shoulders. "He just showed up. He said he'd been thinking about me a lot and decided to come over. It's nice to be at the top of somebody's priority list!"

"Yeah." I brushed back the strands of hair that were sticking to my face. "It must be in the nineties. I wish they hadn't closed the pool."

Sitting up straight in her chair, Breeze looked over her shoulder, as if to make sure that Flynn was out of earshot. "Hayley," she said, "you need to change your shirt."

I wiped my neck. "But I'm only halfway through the lawn. I don't want to stink up another one."

"You can borrow one of mine. How about the Artscape one you like?" she offered.

"Your blue Artscape T-shirt?" I didn't get it. "What does it matter how I look? He's not here to see me."

"Exactly."

"So?"

"So . . . he's mine!"

"Well, they always are," I said.

She rolled her eyes. "You are so naïve, it's unbeliev-able! You're just like Dad. Hayley, there's more than one way to attract a guy. Look at yourself. Just look!"

I glanced down. Okay, the shirt was gaping where the buttons had been—maybe it was gaping a lot. And sweat was making the cotton cling to my skin.

"Why do you think he was looking at you the way he was?"

I felt my cheeks coloring. "Because I'm covered with grass."

"Don't play dumb!"

Just then, Flynn came through the doors to the deck. I flattened the little towel against my chest. Flynn handed us our ice waters, then pulled a third chair over. I thanked him, sat down, and tried to arrange the towel in a casual kind of way, like a girl who had just worked out and flung a towel over her shoulder. But it wasn't long enough, and, the more I tried to cover the gaping and clingy areas, the more I looked like I was wearing a baby bib.

Flynn suddenly turned his head away, but before he did, I saw him laughing. He knew what was going on.

I threw down the towel. "I've got stuff to do," I said, took a gulp of cold water, and stalked off to cut the grass.

7

$\mathcal{I}$t didn't take much to get the school gossips going, and by Monday afternoon whispers of Breeze and Flynn were flying around. I got grilled at the newspaper office.

"Is Flynn chasing Breeze or Breeze chasing Flynn?" Paige asked.

"I have no idea."

"According to several people who were with Breeze in the parking lot after the game, Flynn's chasing her."

"Well, there's your answer," I said, and went back to reading Gabriel's article so I could find the perfect photo for it.

Flynn called our house Tuesday and Wednesday nights

that week. Friday night, he and Breeze planned to meet after the game, and even I was a little curious about whether they would join the famous postgame get-together that was usually held at one of the players' houses. All the cool people were invited. Flynn and Breeze were ultracool, but, of course, Jared would be there *and* Jared was now the one-and-only star of the team, and you couldn't diss him.

Friday night, before the game, as I stood on the sideline checking my equipment, I got a surprise visit from The Star.

"Haaay-ley," he said.

"Jared. What's up?"

"That picture you took last week," he began.

"The one of you we printed in *The Courier*?" It was a fabulous photo, if I do say so myself. Jared was standing on the sideline, helmet off, squeezing a football in his hand, watching the defense. His eyes were on the game, but you got the feeling he was visualizing great plays by himself and the offense. We used the photo with a story that Gabriel wrote about college athletic scholarships.

"Do you think I could have a copy of it?"

"No problem."

"Two?"

"Sure."

"Three?" he asked. "One for my parents, one for my

grandmother, and one for me. My mom and grandmother keep sports scrapbooks for me. Each of their sets starts with T-ball."

"They have scrapbooks about you as a *preschool* athlete?" I tried not to laugh. "Well, okay."

"Would you mind five?" he asked. "You know, in case a friend would want a copy."

"I'll make five. But don't spread it around to the other guys, or else the newspaper office will turn into a photo lab."

"Thanks, Hayley. You're the greatest."

He turned at the same time I did, and we saw Flynn jogging across the field toward us. Flynn's arm was still in a sling, and he held it steady with his left hand. When he was ten feet from us, he said, "Coach is wondering what you're doing over here, Jared."

I glanced across the field.

"Of course, he used different words than that."

Jared laughed, which surprised me. He must have heard the rumors—must have known how quickly his friend had moved in on Breeze—but they got along the way they always had.

Jared flashed me a smile. "Catch you later, Hayley, okay?" He set off at a fast jog and Flynn followed.

Despite the fact that we had home-team advantage, our team played raggedly during the first quarter. In the second quarter, the defense pulled itself together, but the offense struggled until after halftime.

Six minutes into the third quarter, I was kneeling on the ground, rummaging through my camera bag, when I became aware of a small shadow attached to my heel. I glanced over my shoulder. A little girl, maybe five years old, stood quietly, pointing her pink plastic camera toward the players. There was fencing to keep the crowd off the sidelines, although teachers and the parents of players were sometimes allowed onto the grass. The little girl looked familiar, and I figured she was one of the teachers' kids or perhaps a member of a "football family" like Jared's, who attended every game.

She smiled at me shyly.

"Covering the game?" I asked, closing my bag.

She nodded.

"Great camera."

She beamed. "It's a Barbie camera."

"No kidding!"

"It really works," she said. "Want to see?"

I took it from her and looked through the viewfinder. "Wow!"

"It's not a dichal. When I get bigger, Daddy said I can have a dichal."

"Well, digitals are nice, but there is something very

70

special about a Barbie cam." I glanced toward the field, where the players were lining up for the next play. "Listen," I said, "you need to shoot from back there. Sometimes the players come flying over this line. You might get hurt."

She turned toward the stands, then back to the field. "I want a good picture," she replied sweetly, stubbornly. I felt like I was looking at a five-year-old me.

"I know. Trust me, I know! But I don't want you to get clobbered."

"I won't," she said, and knelt down next to me, pointing her camera toward the players.

"What's your name?" I asked.

"Emma."

I rose to my feet and took her hand. "Come on, Emma. I'll show you a great new angle."

I was leading her back toward the first row of bleachers when I saw a blond woman running down the steps toward us.

"Thank you!" she said, as she reached us and took Emma's hand. "Thank you so much. I'm terribly sorry. Her father was taking her and her sister to the hot dog stand, and somehow he lost her."

"No problem. I used to get lost a lot, too. Nice meeting you, Emma."

I continued to photograph the game, which we won by

a field goal with one-point-three seconds left. Everyone from Saylor Mill was ecstatic, everyone except me—field goals do not make very exciting photos.

After the game, the crowd filed out slowly, still buzzing. The night was warm, the stars soft, and the crickets chanting as if it were still summer. People gathered on the grass between the stadium and parking lot, waiting for players to emerge from the locker rooms located beneath the stadium stands. Gabriel was still inside interviewing. Sitting on a brick wall next to Kathleen, I reviewed the photos on my digital.

"Hayley," Kathleen said, nudging me. "Hayley, I think someone wants to talk to you."

I looked up. "Well, hi, Emma."

The little girl giggled the way kindergarteners do, shifting her weight from foot to foot, wanting to talk but unable to think of anything to say. Her camera was hanging around her neck.

"Did you shoot your whole roll?" I asked. "Did you finish your film?"

She nodded and dimpled. "Uh-huh. Can I see your pictures?"

I glanced around. "Does your mom know where you are?"

She pointed off to the right, and her mother waved

at us. I returned the wave, then set down the camera so I could lift Emma onto the wall next to me. Those little hands snatched up that digital faster than I could blink.

"*I'll* hold it," I said, laughing.

I began to click through the photos so she could see them on the LCD. She wanted to be the one to press the button.

"Well, the problem is, this is an awfully expensive camera," I explained.

"Please, Hayley," she said, having shrewdly picked up my name from Kathleen. It worked. I put my arm around her so that my hands would be around her little ones and the camera wouldn't tumble onto the concrete. "Press here."

She was a natural at clicking buttons—aren't all kids?

"Emma!"

Both Emma and I looked up, startled. Flynn stood in front of us, his head cocked slightly, as if asking her what she was up to.

"I saw you on the sideline," he said.

"No, you didn't," Emma replied.

"Yes, I did. Third quarter."

She shook her head so hard, the wisps of blond hair whipped back and forth.

"How many times have I told you that the field is too

dangerous for you during a game?"

"Um . . . I don't know," she told him, then looked down at the camera and started clicking the review button, as if he weren't there.

"*Emma?*"

She ignored him for a moment, then smiled. "Hayley said I could stay there."

"I—What?"

Flynn laughed. "I see. Hayley needed your help?"

"Yes."

"I didn't know you had a little sister," Kathleen said to Flynn.

"Two." He pointed toward the lot. Emma's mother was talking to a tall man, who I figured was their father. Another little girl was hanging from the man's hands, pulling up her feet and trying to swing. "That's Meg," Flynn said, then wiggled the fingers with which he had just pointed. "You don't think I put this on myself!"

Three nails were painted a bright, glittery pink.

"Wow, that must be *Barbie* pink," I said.

"Girlfriend," he replied, batting his eyes at me, waving his hand, "do you wear that color, too?"

Kathleen and I laughed. Emma bent my fingers to look at the nails. "No," she informed him. "She doesn't wear anything."

"Well, she would have to, if she lived in our house." To

me, Flynn said, "I hope Emma didn't mess up your work, Hayley."

"No. Like all photographers, she just wanted to get a good shot."

"Come on," he said to his sister. "Meg is getting whiny."

Emma let go of my fingers, but didn't move. "Give me a ride?"

"Sure, sure, little girl. I'll give you a ride—all the way to the dragon's cave."

Emma squealed and he swooped her up in his left arm, threw her over his shoulder and carried her off to their parents.

"How cute!" Kathleen observed.

"Yeah, she is."

Kathleen burst out laughing. "Yeah, she is, *too*. Here comes Gabe. Let's roll."

"Hey, Dad," I said, twenty minutes later.

He was watching the History Channel in the family room. "Hi, honey. Who won?"

"We did, but it wasn't a good game."

"Oh, well, it will still look good in the paper, especially if that photographer was covering it. What was her name—Barley?"

Ever notice how really smart people enjoy making silly jokes? "Barley or Hayley," I said, setting down my bag,

75

giving him a hug from behind. "Want something from the kitchen?"

"No, thanks."

I was in the kitchen, stacking cheese, tomato, and lettuce on a piece of bread when I heard Breeze and Flynn greet Dad. I quickly took a cold soda from the fridge, not wanting to end up with another flat one that had been hibernating in my bedroom for too long.

"I won't be long. I'm just changing my shirt," Breeze said.

"Hayley's in the kitchen," my father told Flynn. "Go help yourself to whatever you want, Jared."

Like I said, Dad is spacey. Of course, poor guy, just as he gets used to one name, the next boyfriend comes along.

"Hey, Jared," I said as Flynn entered the kitchen.

One side of his mouth pulled up in a sarcastic smile.

"Would you like something to drink? Eat?"

"No, we'll be going in a minute. Breeze is just changing her clothes."

I must have smirked in response.

"What?" he asked.

"Nothing."

"Breeze takes a long time to change a shirt," he guessed.

"It's the first time with you, so she might hurry." I pulled a high stool from beneath the kitchen island, sat down, and took a bite out of my sandwich. For several minutes, I chewed silently and tried hard to read the newspaper. Flynn sat close, choosing a stool that made a corner with mine. I felt his eyes like heat but was determined not to let him see that he was getting to me. I handed him some of the paper. "If you get hungry, let me know."

"Maybe I'll have some ice water," he said. "Don't get up. I'm good at picking out fridges."

I saw the little smirk, then the twinkle in his eyes, and I laughed. "The glasses are over the sink."

When he returned to the island with his water, he pointed to a photo on the front page of the sports section. "Is this what you want to do one day?"

"Be a professional sports photographer? I don't know. I cover other things at school—club activities, dances, you name it. And I didn't start out as a huge sports fan. But I like the challenge of photographing games. The constant motion, the varying light conditions, the need to be in exactly the right spot at exactly the right moment—it's cool."

He smiled, and I went on. "It's not enough for me just to be there for the big play. Kind of like an athlete, I have to have my body positioned perfectly, go in at exactly the right angle."

"That *is* cool," he agreed. "So, do you ever wish you could do a play over again?"

"Oh, yeah! Sometimes a whole game!"

"I know *that* feeling," he said. "Do you ever feel like you do everything right, but it just doesn't work out? And then other times, you're unbelievably lucky, and it all seems so ridiculously easy?"

"Absolutely."

"So when somebody says—I guess to you they would say 'Great photo, Hayley!'—and you feel like it was pure luck, do you take credit for it?"

"I say thanks, and leave it at that. How about you? 'Best game you ever played, Flynn!' But you know deep down . . ."

"I say thanks." He smiled. "And I leave it at that. Do you work better with or without pressure?"

I thought about the question. "I like pressure. I love it when the adrenaline gets pumping. But there is something really nice about taking a walk on an empty beach with my camera, and with nothing but ocean and sky and gulls flying around me, letting the picture come to me."

When he spoke, his voice was soft. "I could enjoy that."

We were both leaning on our elbows. In the shiny granite surface I saw our reflections, saw how we leaned toward each other like friends sharing secrets, and I pulled back.

After a moment Flynn sat back and glanced at his watch, then at the clock on the microwave. He frowned a little. "Breeze knows that the guys are usually tired. The party doesn't go on for that long."

"You're going to the team party?" I asked with surprise.

"Yeah. Why?"

"Nothing," I said quickly.

He studied my face.

"Nothing. Really," I told him, getting up to put my plate in the dishwasher.

"You don't approve. Miss Caldwell doesn't approve."

"Well, it *is* sort of an odd way to show loyalty to a teammate. I mean, you and Jared are good friends. And he and Breeze just broke up. But it's none of my business."

"You're right," Flynn said, his voice suddenly sounding tight. "It is none of your business. But just for the record, I cleared it with Jared first."

"Well, then, great."

Flynn took a long drink of water. "Come on, Hayley, you know how it is. If it wasn't me, some other guy would jump at a chance with Breeze. And she seems very willing."

"I know how it is," I agreed. "I don't understand it, but

I've seen it enough to know how it works."

"So what don't you get?"

"The way people talk and act like they're crazy in love, and then, *ding*, suddenly they're not. It's like it was all just pretend. Like it's just a game."

He crunched on an ice cube. "Well, sometimes it *is* just a game."

"Then how are you supposed to believe someone when it *isn't*?"

He tilted his glass and watched the ice cubes slide around. "I—I don't know."

I poured myself more soda to take to my room.

"I guess you're one of those really honest people," Flynn observed.

"No," I said, after thinking for a moment, "not always."

He laughed. "You just proved my point. So let's say you're honest ninety-nine percent of the time."

"Okay."

"That one percent of the time when you're not," he went on, "what would make you decide not to be?"

I laughed at him. "If you think I'm telling you that, you're crazy."

He shrugged and smiled.

Breeze came into the kitchen then, looking incredible in her beaded top. I wondered if Flynn was thinking what I was thinking: Jared was going to see firsthand what he had given up.

Was Breeze completely over Jared? I wondered. Was she really falling for Flynn—or was she just using him to get to Jared? Well, that was Flynn's problem, not mine.

"Have a good time," I said, and exited the kitchen quickly, forgetting my soda.

8

*L*ate Saturday morning, Breeze was sitting on the edge of my bed, begging. "Please, please, please, Hayley."

"But I told you," I replied, stuffing a pile of clean underwear in my drawer, "a group of us are playing miniature golf tonight."

"Well, if it's a whole group, they won't miss you. What I mean is," she added quickly, "they'll miss you, but they'll have others to hang out with, while you make money. I thought you were saving for a camera."

"And who exactly is going to pay me this money?"

Flynn had to babysit; he had just called to change their

plans for tonight. His parents said that he could invite Breeze over, but Breeze refused to babysit any child who wasn't already asleep. Flynn had warned her that Emma and Meg were allowed to stay up later than usual on Saturday night, and then had jokingly invited her to a "Barbie party." Breeze didn't think it was funny.

"I'll pay you," she said.

"With what? You've blown your September budget. And I don't take credit cards."

Breeze twisted a strand of gold hair around her finger. "I can buy something with my card, then return it, and ask for cash back."

It didn't take a business genius to figure out that, if a store actually allowed that, not only would I get paid for babysitting, my father would then see the charge on the credit card bill and attempt to even things off. But it wasn't fair to Dad. And, while I've never really liked miniature golf, I prickled at the idea that Breeze's social life was more important than mine—even if she were headed for an evening with the gorgeous and cool Flynn, while I was just trying to drive a ball into the grinning mouth of a stupid spinning clown.

"No," I told her firmly.

Fifteen minutes later, the phone rang. Breeze picked it up, then called from her room, "It's for you."

I pushed back from my computer screen and grabbed the phone. "Hello?"

"Hayley?"

"Yes?"

"This is Laura Delancy. I can't tell you how delighted we are that you are willing to babysit Meg and Emma. Emma is beside herself with joy. She's here in the family room now, lining up her dolls to show you."

I pulled the phone away from my ear for a moment and stared at it in disbelief. *Breeze!*

"I'm so glad you're available at such late notice."

I turned toward the door of my room, which faced the door to Breeze's, but she had closed hers most of the way. I assumed she could feel my laser stare even through the wood.

"Tom, my husband, will pick you up at seven fifteen. Now, tell me, what do you like to eat? Of course, you are welcome to anything already in the refrigerator, but we want to make sure we have something you like."

"Uh—"

"Excuse me just a moment, Hayley." Then she said in a calm, motherly voice, "No, not now, girls. There will be plenty of time to talk to Hayley tonight."

I was going to kill Breeze.

"As you can tell," she said to me, "they're both very

excited that you're coming."

Now how was I supposed to say no? Sure, I could explain that my sister must not have heard me correctly. But I really hate to disappoint people. I guess I'm a wuss!

When I got off the phone, I heard Breeze's door inching open. She peeked around it, then emerged. "Thanks, Hayley, I—"

I rose quickly from my chair. "Don't even talk to me," I said, and slammed my door in her face.

As I found out later, Flynn had offered to take Breeze to Panera's for dinner before they babysat, so now that the babysitting was covered, they were going for both an early dinner and a movie. Flynn arrived ten minutes early for the date, which meant he'd be hanging around our house for twenty-five minutes or more. I usually answered the front door for Breeze's dates because Dad didn't have a clue how to make conversation with the guys. But I hid in my room, deciding that Dad and Flynn—or Jared, as he'd probably call him—would have to make the best of it.

Dad had heard the door slam earlier in the day and had noticed that he was left to entertain tonight's date. As we sat down to our Saturday night favorite, Royal Farm rotisserie chicken, he asked, "How's everything?"

"Fine."

He waited—not prompting, just waiting. I finally gave in to the silence and told him I had changed plans and was going to babysit for the Delancys.

He nodded. "Jared's family."

"Flynn's," I corrected. "The guy you answered the door for, his name is Flynn."

"Maybe I should write that down," Dad replied, and pulled a small notebook from his shirt pocket to scribble down the name.

It was hard to stay mad that night, between my sweet, spacey father and the warm welcome the Delancys gave me. Since I had made no special request for food, they had bought brownies and cold cuts, but Dr. Delancy offered to stop at the store on the way to their house. I told him brownies were perfect.

When we walked in the door, the little girls danced around me, then each one grabbed a hand to lead me to the family room. Even the house made me feel happy. It was old, made of stone and clapboard on the outside, a kind of overgrown cottage. On the inside it had polished wood floors, bright colored rugs, comfy chairs, and lots of pretty stuff like flowered wallpaper and silver candlesticks.

The family room was at the end of a hall and next to

the kitchen. In a whirlwind of five minutes, I learned the names of an assortment of Barbie dolls, baby dolls, and stuffed animals, along with important telephone numbers, and what was and wasn't allowed. Then Dr. and Mrs. Delancy drove off, and the girls and I settled down to play Barbies. After that we colored and then played a board game, but most of the night was spent being princesses.

Mrs. Delancy had given Meg and Emma a box of cosmetics. Some containers appeared to be her old stuff, while others were designed for little girls. Before leaving she had said that the girls were allowed to put on the cosmetics, as long as everything but the nail polish was cleaned off before bed.

Sitting on the closed lid of the toilet in the downstairs bathroom, we took turns getting powdered. My face got so many coats, I looked like I had run into a sack of flour. Blush was applied. When Meg didn't think my cheeks were pink enough, she spit on the container of red granules, ground her finger in it, and pressed it into my cheeks. Emma, who tended to follow her older sister's lead, did the same. Glancing at myself in the mirror, I saw a circus clown with round red patches for cheeks.

I let them apply my eye shadow, purple on one lid, green on the other, since they couldn't agree which was best—Emma herself wore green and Meg, purple. All three of us put on bright pink lipstick. Each of the girls had a fake-jewel tiara to wear. They made me a paper crown, which was crusted over with glitter and a little lopsided. I bobby-pinned it on.

Exhausted from all this beauty work, we took a break and ate brownies. The girls asked to put on their nightgowns—because, of course, they were *gowns*—then we returned to the first-floor bathroom to put on glitter nail polish.

"Wow, we're so pretty!" I said, hardly able to keep a straight face, as we stood in front of the vanity mirror admiring ourselves.

"Yes, we are," Emma replied seriously.

The girls asked to watch a video. When they gave me very specific directions, I realized that this was a bedtime ritual. We had to sit on the love seat, not the sofa, spread the blue afghan on our laps, and lower the lights just so. I was told I could put my feet up on the coffee table "like Mommy." The girls snuggled against me, one on each side, lifting my hands so that my arms would be wrapped around them. We were so comfy, I was afraid I would fall asleep.

We had been nestled together for about twenty minutes, the girls' curly eyelashes fluttering closed beneath their crowns, when I remembered the rule about removing makeup. Just as I put the video on pause, I heard the front door open. I glanced at my watch: ten o'clock—I thought that Mrs. Delancy had said midnight. The hall light came on, footsteps sounded on the floor, and a moment later, Flynn entered. He stopped about ten feet from his sisters and me, studied us a moment, and burst out laughing. That woke them up.

"Hello, princesses."

"Hi, Flynn," Emma said, sitting up.

When she threw open her arms, he leaned down and gave her a hug. Meg opened her arms, and she, too, got a warm hug. I wondered what would happen if I tried it, but, of course, I didn't.

"Are we pretty?" Meg asked.

"You are beautiful," Flynn replied. "I've never seen three such beautiful princesses."

"Have you seen many princesses of any kind?" I asked, and he laughed.

"What are you watching?"

"Barbie," replied Meg. "*Swan Lake.*"

"A classic," Flynn observed. "Are you enjoying it, Hayley?"

"Actually, I was," I admitted. "How was your movie?"

"Okay. It was a chick flick."

"Well, what do you think this one is?"

He smiled. "A baby chick flick."

"We're not babies," Emma cried indignantly.

He held up his hand. "Sorry. Sorry, I know that. You're big girls." To me he said, "I guess you had them almost asleep before I barged in."

"That's okay. I need to wash off their makeup."

"No!" cried Meg, disappointed.

"I have to keep it on," Emma insisted. "I want to have princess dreams."

"You will," Flynn assured Emma. "Just look at your Cinderella light as you fall asleep. Come on."

It was obvious that Flynn was used to taking care of the girls. He led the way to the downstairs bathroom, then got out cold cream, a box of baby wipes, and a fresh washcloth—"in case we have to scrub," he said to me. He set to work on Meg while I washed Emma. "Sit still, Meg, I've got just one hand."

I peeked sideways at him, fascinated by the deft and gentle way he removed the makeup. When the girls were both fairly clean—their lips still shone pinkish—he turned to me. "Next."

"What?"

"Don't tell me. You're going to throw a hissy fit because you want to keep your makeup on."

"Well, noooo."

"I'll wash you," Emma said.

"And me," Meg insisted.

They each took a cheek.

"No, not her eyes, not with that!" Flynn said, catching Meg's hand. "Close your eyes," he told me, then carefully wiped my lids. "Jeez, how many layers did you girls put on?"

When he had stopped wiping my eyes, I opened them and found him looking intently at me. For one long moment we gazed at each other. It seemed as if everything else in the room faded away. The expression on his face was unlike any I'd ever caught with my camera. Then he pulled back and stuffed the damp cloth in my hand. "I don't know why I'm doing this. You're old enough." He dried his hand on a towel. "Come on, girls, let's choose some books and give Hayley private time in the bathroom."

I finished wiping my face, removed my crown, then joined them on the love seat. Flynn sat on the right side, so that his injured arm wouldn't get bumped, I sat on the left, and the girls squeezed in the middle. Once again, my arm was tugged on and arranged around their shoulders. Flynn laid his good arm along the back of the seat. With the afghan spread over our laps, Emma and Meg turned the pages of the picture books while Flynn and I took turns reading.

It was cozy, but this time I was in no danger of falling asleep, not with the nerve endings in my shoulder doing strange, dancy things. Flynn's arm had slipped off the top edge of the love seat and his hand rested on my shoulder. Every time Meg moved, my hand, caught between her and Flynn, got pressed against his ribs. Both Flynn and I had our feet up on the coffee table. He stretched out his long legs, and I pulled mine back. I imagined that if our feet touched, it would be like closing a circuit, and he might feel the odd kind of electricity that was running through me.

At the end of the fourth book, Flynn said, "It's time for all princesses to go to their tower room."

The girls must have been tired, because they didn't resist. Emma took my hand and we followed Flynn and Meg upstairs to a room with a sloping ceiling, dormer windows, and twin beds with rose-patterned spreads.

Meg lit the Cinderella nightlight so that it glowed warmly. Flynn turned out the bureau lamp, and the three of them knelt down along the side of a bed. I suddenly realized what we were doing and joined the lineup. We prayed for Mommy, Daddy, Flynn, Flynn's arm, me, their kindergarten and first-grade teachers, the football team, and Hazel, Mrs. Korbet's old dog, which had worms.

"Will they have to kill the worms?" Emma asked, when we were finished.

"Yes," Flynn replied, "but the worms don't feel anything."

We added a prayer for the souls of the worms.

After that, there were good-night hugs from Flynn and me. "We're kind of a huggy family," he explained, as two little arms wrapped around me.

Flynn gestured for me to go out and pulled the door closed three quarters of the way. When we reached the first floor, he said, "I bet you've never prayed for worms before."

"No. I've never prayed for the football team, either."

"You haven't? Hayley, I'm disappointed in you."

For a moment I thought he was serious, then I saw his eyes grow brighter—I saw a smile that shone in his eyes before it made it to the sweet curve of his mouth.

"Maybe that's why we're doing so badly," he said.

"We're doing badly because you're not playing."

He led the way back to the family room. "No. Really, that's not it," he told me. "Gavin has a lot of talent, and once he gets some confidence, things will change. I just hope the fans don't get on him too soon."

"He's good, but he's not—"

"Trust me, if they give him a chance, I'm going to have to bust my butt to get my position back next year." He sat down on the love seat and put his feet up on the coffee table.

"Gabriel said that it was a really tough time for you to get injured," I began, not knowing how much to say. Maybe he didn't want me to act like I knew it was the worst possible time in terms of college scholarships. Maybe he'd be insulted by my sympathy.

"Yeah, well, it's part of the game."

"A painful part," I said.

His eyes flicked away for a moment. "Yeah." Then he turned to me. "Are you going to sit down? I can't take you home now. We can't leave the girls."

"Oh. Oh, right. Sure." I backed up—kept backing up till I felt the leather of the large sofa behind my knees, then sat. He laughed.

"I wish you wouldn't do that," I blurted out.

"Do what?"

"Laugh, when I haven't made a joke, like I'm funny or something."

"You are funny, Hayley."

I glowered at him, or tried to.

"In a good way. It's just hard to talk to you all the way over there. That's why I was laughing."

"Well . . . well, you took the left side of the love seat, and I don't want to have to sit on your right side because I might accidentally bump your arm. You know, if I hurt you, Siefert will put a contract out on me."

He smiled. "Okay," he said, and joined me on the leather sofa, the right side. He carried the remote control with him. "You can pick up with Barbie or find something else. Your choice. I'm going to make some popcorn. There must be brownies out there—they always get brownies for the babysitters."

I nodded.

"Want anything else? Something to drink? Milk? Coke? I'll bring both, you can't have milk with popcorn." A few minutes later he emerged carrying a tray with the food, along with a bottle of Coke, a bottle of milk, two plates and four glasses. I laughed.

"I wish you wouldn't do that," he said, mimicking me.

He set the tray on a table next to me, took what he wanted, then slid past me and sat down, putting his feet up on another of the Delancys' battered coffee tables. I had turned on the rebroadcast of Maryland's football game. Gabriel and I had watched a lot of football games side by side, and I'd never once noticed how we sat. But all I could think about now was that Flynn had seated himself just eight inches away, leaving a lot of sofa on the other side of him. I tried to concentrate on the game, but I found myself staring at Flynn's shoes, wondering strange things, like what his feet looked like.

"Are they in your way?" Flynn asked.

"What?" I asked, surprised.

"My feet. I know they're huge, but I didn't think they were blocking your view."

"Oh, no, no, they aren't. I was just wondering . . ." My voice trailed off. *Way to go, Hayley! Now what was I going to say?*

"Wondering?"

"Uh, if your sisters painted your toes, too."

Flynn laughed. "Actually, they did, hoping to improve them. I have very ugly jock feet."

"Let's see." It had popped out of my mouth before I could stop it.

Flynn's eyes glittered with laughter. "You want to see my feet?"

"Never mind." *Jeez, Hayley.*

I could feel him studying me, then, using the toe of one shoe against the heel of the other, he flipped off a Docksider. "You asked for it," he warned, and removed his sock.

I looked at his foot and burst out laughing.

"Excuse me," Flynn said, feigning hurt. "*Excuse* me. I had hoped for a more polite response."

"It *is* a funny foot," I said. "And the pink-sparkle nails don't help much."

"All right, let's see yours."

"What?"

"Fair is fair. I want to see your feet."

"Well . . . well . . . they look just like Breeze's," I said.

"I don't think so," he replied. "Because hands usually match feet, and, even though the rest of you is the same size as Breeze, your fingers are longer than hers."

I blinked. He was right, but I was surprised he'd noticed that.

He reached and tugged on my shoelace. When I didn't move, he untied it. He glanced back at me then gently slipped off my sneaker.

I pulled back my foot. I felt suddenly and unbelievably shy. *It's just a stupid foot, Hayley,* I told myself. But somehow, this felt so personal. Despite the fact that a million people had seen my bare feet at the pool, Flynn staring at one of them made me feel very vulnerable.

"Well?" he said.

I realized there was something even worse than me removing my sock: Flynn removing it. I took it off. "There."

"Very pretty," he said. "You have very nice, dainty toes."

I quickly tugged on my sock.

Flynn laughed out loud, then put on his sock and Docksider. I focused on tying my shoe.

"Mind if we watch *Saturday Night Live?*" he asked.

After a few minutes and a lot of laughing from Flynn, I began to relax again. For some reason, the skits seemed terribly funny that night, funnier than they ever had before. Once I started laughing, I couldn't stop. I noticed that, sometimes, Flynn laughed just because I had.

A clock in the hall struck twelve. Five minutes later, Mr. and Mrs. Delancy unlocked the front door. I frowned at my watch, unable to believe they had already come home, feeling for a moment like Cinderella.

And maybe that should have been a warning to me.

"It's about time! Where were you?"

I had tried to be quiet, in case Breeze was in bed, but she was leaning against the wide entrance to the family room, her arms folded, one hand holding a remote. Behind her, the TV screen showed the menu for the DVD she must have been watching.

"What?"

"Where were you?"

"Babysitting. You got me the job, remember?"

"Flynn left here two hours ago."

I nodded. "He came straight home."

"So why didn't you?"

Now I understood, but I guess I was still pretty annoyed with her. "*Because* I was babysitting. Are you having short-term memory loss?"

"Since Flynn was home, the Delancys didn't need you."

"Yes, but he couldn't drive me home and leave the little girls alone. And it was too late to put them in his car while he dropped me off. So I stayed till his parents arrived."

Breeze tapped the remote against her thigh. "It wasn't too late to call me."

I frowned, then glanced away. The idea had never occurred to me.

"You've called for a ride home from Gabriel's plenty of times. And don't tell me that you stayed as late as you could simply because you wanted to earn more money."

"Well, that's a good reason," I said.

She scowled. "You're the most ridiculously honest person in all of Saylor Mill. If you had thought of that angle, you would have called a taxi and paid for it yourself!"

"I would *not* have paid for it," I insisted. "I'd have figured out what was less expensive for the Delancys, either paying for my taxi or paying for extra hours, and chosen according to that."

She rolled her eyes, and I couldn't really blame her. "I

guess I didn't think about calling because I was having a good time—the girls are very cute," I added quickly.

"And when did they go to bed?" she asked.

"Breeze, stop! Stop it! Put your brain back on. Go look in a mirror. Reread your diary. We both know which of us all the guys fall for. You've got nothing to worry about."

She studied me quietly for a moment, biting her lip. "You've got glitter on your face."

I brushed my cheek. It felt warm, like I was blushing. "I'm really tired, Breeze. G'night."

Some people wouldn't understand why I'd do a favor for Breeze after she was acting so huffy the night before. But those people probably have more than just one sister and one parent—a parent whose mind can stray as far as Pluto. Breeze and I have been through everything together, and sometimes you just have to forget about who's right and who's wrong, and put up with each other's silliness. Or maybe it was just that I needed to put Flynn back into a "photograph"—slip him into a frame where he would be nothing more to me than a two-dimensional image.

In any case, when I sat down at my computer Sunday afternoon to work on the picture that Jared had requested, I asked Breeze if she wanted to look with me through photos of Flynn and select two that I could print for her.

She chose one of those "vision on the sideline" photos that people seem to like, probably because the players have their helmets off and their faces are more visible. I would have chosen it, too. But Breeze's lips curled with disdain when she saw one of my favorite photos of Flynn, which I had taken at last year's spring dance. He was standing with Nicole, his arm around her, smiling right into the camera's eye.

"You've got to admit it's a great shot of him," I said.

"Yeah." She lifted her hand to block out Nicole. "*Yeah*. The problem is, if you cut her out, it will look like his arm's been amputated. Maybe you could crop it so it shows just his neck and face."

"I'll see what I can do."

"Thanks, Hayley." She wandered off to do homework and some beautifying regimen, and I set to work, improving the lighting in the photo that Jared had requested, then saving it so it would be ready for the school printer, which was better than mine. When I began my work on Flynn's pictures, I had a sudden inspiration and headed for the collection of old photo albums shelved in our family room. I counted the years backward and found the album that contained our trip to Sesame Place.

Back in my room, I removed one of the pictures. Dad has told me that when Mom went into the darkroom, she would completely lose track of time. Well, when I started fooling with Photoshop, the same thing happened.

Sometime later, Breeze knocked on my door, then entered. "I thought maybe you had fallen asleep in here."

"Just putting the final touches on Flynn's picture," I said, and pushed back from my desk, so she could see the screen. "How do you like it?"

Breeze leaned down for a better look, then threw back her head and laughed, then nearly strangled me with a hug from behind. "I love it! Love it!"

Monday, when I passed Jared in the hall, I told him I'd be printing copies of his photo and would give them to him tomorrow. That day it rained, and rained, and rained—a nor'easter was moving through. After school, Paige and I were hanging around the newspaper office, waiting to hitch a ride with Kathleen.

I had finished Jared's photos and gone as far as I could with the photos for Friday's edition—sports pictures, a picture of the drama club with Nicole hamming it up, and the debate club. Sitting at our long conference table, I worked on my geometry homework. Kathleen was writing a history paper. With four little brothers at home, she could get a lot more done here. Paige was working on her novel, a romance with so many love stories going on readers needed a program with a team roster. Everyone else had left, and there was a peaceful feeling in the office, with just the sounds of my scratchy pencil, their tapping keys, and the rain against the windows.

"Haaay-ley!"

All three of us looked up.

"Hi, Jared," Kathleen said, then went back to typing.

Paige smiled and cocked her head a little, studying Jared, who had come in looking soaked and cute. I had the feeling he had just earned himself a walk-on part in her novel. She typed a sentence, then looked up at him again, as steadily as a person painting his portrait. Jared didn't mind. He paused to smile back at her, holding that smile, like an experienced politician who gives the media time to snap his photo.

I went back to my math problem.

"Haaay-ley," he repeated, realizing he had lost my attention.

"Is practice over already?" I asked.

"Yeah, with the field so bad, we did just weights and machines today. We can't risk losing somebody else to an injury."

I nodded, and he sat down across from me. His blond hair was dark with rain and wavy with the moisture. His blues sparkled at me.

"I bet you're here for your pictures."

"And to see you," he said.

Beyond his right shoulder, I saw Paige's eyes rise above her monitor.

"Let me get them for you," I told him, shoving back from the table in my wheeled chair, gliding back to the shelf where I had set them.

I opened the folder in front of him and spread out the copies. I had made two 8 x 12s, figuring his grandmother and parents might like that, three 4 x 5s, and, as a little bonus, four wallet-sized.

"Wow!" he said.

Perhaps he was complimenting my work, but there was something funny about a guy staring down at his own face in multiple forms, saying *Wow!* I bit my lip trying not to laugh.

"Thanks, Hayley, they're great."

"Do you have a pack that will keep them dry?" I asked. "Let me look for some cardboard to protect them." I started to get up, but he grabbed my hand. "I miss you, Hayley."

"What?"

He held on to my hand. Paige's eyes rose again above the horizon of her monitor. This time, so did Kathleen's.

"I miss seeing you."

Paige stopped typing; Kathleen's clicking slowed.

I pulled my hand away. "You see me all the time, taking

pictures on the sideline. I'm not at practice as much as I used to be, now that school has begun, but—"

"I miss hanging out with you."

"Oh, of course." I got up, walked to our stash of packaging material, then pulled out some cardboard and a large envelope. "You mean at my house, while you were waiting for Breeze."

"Yeah. It was fun."

So, he was getting lonely. He was looking for company. Perhaps he was looking for an invitation back to Breeze's house. He had finally realized the mistake he'd made when he dumped her.

"I always liked the shows we watched," he said.

"Don't you get cable at home?" I asked.

I saw Paige grimace and shake her head.

He laughed. "Of course. I just really miss being around you." He sounded so sincere, for a moment I almost believed him.

"Well, thanks," I told him, and quickly slipped the cardboard and his pictures into the envelope. "Keep them dry, okay? You may want to leave them in your locker until the rain clears. I hope your family likes them."

"Oh, they will! I pointed you out to my parents at the game the other night. I told them your name."

"And remember," I went on, as if he hadn't said that,

"keep the fact that I did this for you among family and special friends. I don't have time to print pictures of all the players."

"Oh, sure! I really appreciate your doing something special, *just for me*."

"Right. Bye."

He picked up his envelope, then his pack. "See you soon," he said, smiling at me, then turning to smile at Paige and Kathleen.

As the sound of his footsteps disappeared down the hall, Paige stood up. "Hayley, I think I need to explain some things to you."

"You don't need to explain a thing," I answered quickly. "I have been Breeze's sister since her first boyfriend in fourth grade."

"Yes, but I think that you may not realize that—"

"I know all the tactics," I said.

"Just listen for a moment—"

"Drop it!"

"So why don't we get our stuff together?" Kathleen interjected. "I'm at a stopping point in my paper."

Paige plopped back down in her chair. "But I've got a whole new blast of inspiration!" she protested.

"Jot down your ideas," replied Kathleen. "The old VW departs in five minutes."

Thank you, I mouthed to her, as Paige rattled away on her keyboard.

The next day, after dialing the combination for Breeze's locker and pulling open the metal door, I admired the photographs of Flynn that I had made for her. An old one of Jared was still stuck near the bottom, and it looked like some nail polish had dripped on him. I placed a bag lunch on top of Breeze's jumble of books, hair fixings, and shoes. Earlier, she had passed me in the hall and asked for money, saying she had left her lunch at home. I had paid for enough of her lunches to know I'd never see that money again, but I didn't want her to starve. So I left her my lunch. If we were spending my money, I was going to be the one eating pizza, and she, the bologna and cheese.

As I began to close her locker door, I heard Flynn's voice calling from the next classroom down, "Hayley, wait, I have something to put in there."

Last spring, out of sheer necessity, I had made a rule about me giving other people access to my sister's locker. I shut the door and reset the lock. "Sorry, you have to slip it through the slot, or hand it to her yourself, like everybody else," I told him when he reached me.

"Everybody but you?" he replied.

"Special sister privileges."

He laughed. "I see."

"Do you?"

"Yes. You don't like playing UPS."

I nodded.

"The problem is," he said, "a book won't fit through the slot, and I think she needs it right after lunch."

I glanced down at Breeze's chemistry text.

"I don't know how I ended up with it," he added.

It was my turn to laugh. Misplacing her belongings was one of Breeze's favorite ways of getting a guy to look for her.

"What?" he said, sounding defensive. Apparently it was all right for him to find me funny, but not for me to think he was.

"Okay, you win," I said, and dialed the combination.

I lifted up the lunch so he could place the book beneath it. When I started to close the locker, he caught the door. He had seen his two photos. He looked for a moment at the serious one, then his eyes dropped down to the one taken at last year's dance. There he was, looking gorgeous, cool, happy—his arm around Sesame Street's Big Bird. I had worked hard on the details, making my replacement of Nicole absolutely seamless, and adding little yellow feathers here and there, like on Flynn's pants. For nearly a minute, he studied it seriously, then he leaned back against the lockers and laughed and laughed.

"It's fantastic! It's perfect! Hayley, you're a wizard."

I shrugged.

Flynn crouched down for a moment to look at the photo of Jared that was dripped with fingernail polish, then straightened up. "So who's hanging in your locker?"

"Mine? Uh, Ansel Adams."

"And?" Flynn prompted.

"And he was a great American photographer."

"I know who Ansel Adams is," Flynn said, smiling.

And *I* knew that Flynn was being nosy, asking what current guy I might admire enough to hang in my locker. But I wasn't telling him there was only dead Ansel.

He gave up. "When you get a chance, would you mind making me a copy of my picture with Big Bird? Meg and Emma will love it. No hurry—I know you've been making a lot of photos for Jared."

"He told you that?"

"He showed them to me."

"But I asked him not to tell anyone but his family and special friends."

"Well, I'm a special friend."

"You're the guy hitting on his ex-girlfriend."

The moment I said it, I wanted to jump inside the locker

and pull the door closed.

Flynn stopped smiling. "That really bothers you, doesn't it."

What bothered me even more was the fact that it *really* bothered me—the fact that I wanted so badly for Flynn not to be a typical thoughtless stud. I scuffed my toe against the wall at the base of the locker. "I guess if it doesn't bother Jared, it would be pretty stupid for it to bother me."

Flynn didn't reply and I finally looked up, meeting his eyes. He looked away, the first time he'd ever dodged my gaze, then he turned his attention back to the photos, this time studying the serious one. "You're really good, Hayley."

I nodded. "Yeah. It's the one thing I do well."

"Not the only thing," he said. "You make it sound like it's the only thing."

"I didn't mean it that way." He was making me self-conscious. I closed the door and locked it. "My mother was a photojournalist. I guess it's in the genes."

"You have her eyes," he replied.

"No."

"You don't?"

"My eyes are brown, like my father's. My mother's eyes were a beautiful green, like Breeze's."

"But you have what's important, you have your mother's way of seeing," Flynn said, his voice soft.

"I—I guess so. I gotta run. I really gotta run." Out of the corner of my eye, I saw Gabriel about twenty feet ahead. "Gabriel! Gabe!" I called. "I forgot all about the meeting. Wait up." I hurried toward him.

"What meeting?" he asked, when I reached him.

"Shhh."

He glanced over his shoulder.

"It was just an excuse."

"Oh. I get it," he said.

I suppose it was the terrible self-consciousness I felt and a lot of pent-up frustration: I laughed like a hyena. "No, you don't. You're as clueless as I am, at least about *some* stuff."

"Girl and guy stuff? I know more than you realize," Gabriel replied.

"Oh, really."

"For instance," he said, glancing behind us again, watching Flynn who was talking to two cheerleaders. "I know your cheeks aren't that pink because of *me*."

10

Either Flynn was a little slow to catch on to Breeze's idea of time, or he thought he could retrain her. Wednesday evening he showed up twenty minutes early for his study date with Breeze. He found himself entertained by me and Mrs. Klein, who spent most of the time muttering about the fact that Breeze would miss the dinner she had so carefully prepared. Then Flynn joined me and Dad as we sucked down the soggy noodles of an unbelievably bad tuna casserole. Perhaps his large serving of Tuna Delight helped Flynn to see the situation more clearly. On Thursday evening he and Breeze had their first phone squabble, the topic being his refusal to pick her up before Friday night's game.

From what I could hear, as I bent over my biology book at my bedroom desk, Flynn wanted to be in the locker room early with the team. And he had come to realize he couldn't count on Breeze to be ready. Breeze, of course, was insulted. Her voice rose the way it used to with Jared. "But you're not even playing! . . . What difference does it make? . . . Seifert's a control freak!"

Friday evening Breeze hitched a ride to the game with Kathleen, Jenny, and me. She wasn't a happy camper, especially after Kathleen made her put her makeup on in the girls' bathroom, rather than the newspaper office. "In *that* lighting?!" Breeze gasped.

Kathleen smiled and nodded.

Gabriel and I hooked up and headed over to the stadium. We discussed the game, what we expected to see in the opposing team, et cetera, but he seemed preoccupied.

"New shirt?" I asked, just before we parted at the sideline. Gabriel always wore the same tannish one to games, an L.L. Bean–type like mine.

"Uh, yeah, I guess so," he said, looking down at it, as if he had forgotten what he'd put on.

But he hadn't, I could tell that by his voice, so now I stepped back to study the shirt. It was black with silver lettering: BALTIMORE FILM FESTIVAL. "Cool."

He shrugged as if the shirt was insignificant—he was a terrible actor—and headed across the field toward the players' bench. *Film festival,* I thought. *Jenny. Could it be?*

I was mulling over this possibility when I was suddenly attacked from behind. Two sets of short arms wrapped around my hips. I looked down and saw that my ambushers were wearing tiaras. "Princess Meg, Princess Emma. You're looking quite stunning tonight."

I took several photos of them while they told me their news: They were getting a kitten.

"If it's a girl, we're calling her Princess," Meg said.

"And if it's a boy, then Prince?"

"No, Fang," said Emma. "Flynn gets to choose, if it's a boy."

I kept the girls with me until Mrs. Delancy caught up with them, as I knew she would. When I turned back to the field, I was surprised to find Jenny standing on the sideline, her straight black hair blowing and shining in the breeze. At games, Jenny enjoyed watching the people in the stands more than the athletes. She didn't pursue kids like Paige, trying to wheedle gossip out of them; she just watched them like—well, like she was viewing a movie.

"What's up?"

"I was thinking about after the game," Jenny said. "Want to go out and get something to eat? If Kathleen doesn't want to, you and Gabe could just come to my house, and my mom could drive you home later."

Me and *Gabe* . . . Her cheeks colored as she spoke. If she started wearing a T-shirt that said ESPN ZONE, I'd know for sure.

"Okay."

I watched Jenny skip off to find Kathleen, and I sighed. The team captains gathered for the coin toss, I lifted my camera, and sighed again. I must have been sighing loudly when Gabriel materialized at my elbow.

"I wouldn't give up yet," he said.

I turned to him. "Excuse me?"

"I think we're going to win this game."

"Oh. Right. By the way, Jenny said she'd like to get something to eat after the game."

I peeked sideways at him, but his face showed no expression, and he carefully kept his eyes on the officials and players at the center of the field. "You mean with just you?" he asked.

Gabriel would never have thought something *that* dumb last year. "Yeah, Gabriel, just me and Jenny and Kathleen. No boys allowed."

He nodded solemnly.

"I'm kidding you. Kidding! With all of us, of course!"
He's in deep, I thought.

His face brightened. I sighed, this time, silently.

"You know I can't help but respect Flynn," Gabriel said. My eyes shifted to the opposite side of the field. Flynn was standing with Gavin, his replacement, talking and gesturing, looking like a coach. "He's been working hard with Gavin. He's there every day at practice, coaching him and being positive. Flynn's really a team player. You know, I can get kind of cynical about jocks, but he's really a great person."

"Yeah," I said.

Gabriel turned to me. "What's wrong with you? You sound depressed."

"What's wrong with *me*?" I shot back. "You're the one wearing a strange T-shirt. Who are you trying to impress?"

Well, that did it. We kept our distance from each other, covering the rest of the game fifteen yards apart.

I felt bad for jumping down his throat. It was just that watching Gabriel and Jenny was making me miserable. I could no longer deny what the heat in my cheeks meant when I was around Flynn. It meant the same thing as the pink faces of Gabriel and Jenny, only they were happily falling for each other, and I was falling for my sister's boyfriend.

Get back in your picture frame, I wanted to shout at Flynn.

At the end of halftime, while I was taking the last few gulps of my soda, Flynn trotted across the field. I stood there, my feet planted like tree roots.

"Hayley."

"Flynn."

"I have a message from Jared."

"Don't tell me. He wants another photo."

Flynn smiled. "He wants to know if you'd come to the players' party after the game. It's at his house."

"Oh!"

"You look surprised," Flynn said.

"Well, I am surprised. Don't play dumb, Flynn. You know that only the cool and the beautiful go."

"Maybe *you're* the one thinking dumb," Flynn replied.

I glanced at him, then looked away, still wishing he'd turn back into a photograph. "Anyway, I can't come. I already have plans with my newspaper friends."

"And you're not the kind of girl who ditches a person to accept a better offer."

"Typical jock!" I scoffed. "What makes you think that hanging with the football team is a better offer than hanging with my newspaper friends?"

Flynn blinked, then his cheeks flushed. "You've got a

point," he said, and headed back across the field.

Well, I was doing a terrific job of alienating everyone tonight. I should have taken Flynn's statement as a compliment—that was probably how he had meant it.

At the end of the third quarter, when our team was well ahead in the game, Flynn came back across the field. For a moment we looked at each other warily.

"I have another message," he said. "Jared would like you and all your newspaper friends to come to his party."

I didn't know what to say. Gabriel had always wanted to be invited to that party. I realized he might want to look cool hanging out with the jocks in front of Jenny. As I thought the situation through, I glanced across the field and saw Siefert standing with his hands on his hips, glaring at Flynn and me.

"Siefert's sending daggers," I said.

Flynn turned to look. "That's all right. We're cool, he and I."

"Well, isn't that wonderful," I replied. "You and Siefert are cool. And so are Jared and Siefert. But has it ever occurred to either of you that I have worked my butt off to earn my right to be at practices and photograph the team, and *I* can't afford to be in Siefert's black book? Tell Jared to stop sending his blasted messages across the field to me!"

Flynn took a step back. "Gladly," he replied, then

returned to the bench side.

I bit my lip, then kicked unhappily at the chalky sideline. I was going to get Flynn Delancy back into his picture frame if it meant building one around him.

I guessed that my message got through to Jared, because that was the last I saw of Flynn during the game. Afterward, as Jenny, Kathleen, and I gathered outside the stadium, Gabriel joined us and said excitedly, "Guess what, everybody? Jared just cornered me in the locker room and asked me to invite you all to his party. Want to go?"

"*I* want to go," said Paige, who, having some kind of sixth sense that told her when something was brewing, had appeared almost magically next to Kathleen. "Let me tell Dillon. He's my ride."

Kathleen considered the invitation. "I've always wondered what one of those parties was like. And it's free food," she pointed out practically.

"Let's go!" Jenny said enthusiastically.

Having told Flynn I wanted to be with my newspaper friends, I couldn't suddenly desert them.

We checked in with our parents by cell phone, then hung out in the parking lot until the players emerged and set off for the party. Gabriel had been given directions.

Jared's home was a flat, sprawling house that looked as if it had been almost completely furnished by IKEA.

In the basement there was a Ping-Pong table, pool table, big-screen entertainment center, exercise equipment, and several non-IKEA sofas that looked as if they'd survived years of abuse.

There were a few couples that hung out together, but this was definitely a team event, and the cheerleaders and girlfriends of jocks tended to drift about in all-girl groups. Parents kept arriving downstairs with platters of cold cuts. I made myself a sandwich but barely got through it. Watching the huge slabs of meat get sucked down like yogurt by team members was enough to turn me into a vegetarian.

I saw Breeze before she saw me, talking with two other girls. Her arm was extended, one finger slipped through Flynn's belt loop. When the girls moved on, she glanced over at me with surprise. "Hayley! How did you get here?"

"I came with Kathleen and the others."

Flynn, who had been talking to several teammates and pulling Breeze's arm like a dog on a leash, ended his conversation and turned toward us. "Hayley," he said, but without smiling. I hadn't realized it before, but he usually smiled when he said my name.

"Flynn," I replied, sounding as prickly as he.

"So who invited you?" Breeze asked curiously.

"Jared. He asked the whole group of us to come."

She thought about this for a moment. "Why?"

Flynn glanced sideways at her.

"I haven't a clue."

At that, I saw Flynn's eyes flick up over my shoulder. That was the only warning I got, the only thing that kept me from jumping a mile when I suddenly felt an arm around my waist and a guy's rib cage crushing my left shoulder.

"You made it," Jared said.

I looked up at him curiously.

He gave my arm a squeeze. "I was really afraid you wouldn't come, Hayley."

I glanced toward Breeze. She was a good actress, but I knew her well enough to see the slight narrowing of her eyes. Flynn watched Jared and me thoughtfully, but gave no hint of what he was thinking.

As for Jared, he had eyes for no one but me. "Did you get something to eat?" he asked. "Let me take you upstairs so you can get something from a tray that hasn't been mauled by wild animals."

"Thanks, but I've already had a sandwich." I was trying not to get mad. I was trying hard to believe that Jared was just being friendly, but I suspected he was doing this to get back at Breeze.

"Listen," Jared said, his hand dropping from my waist,

skillfully finding my loose hand and taking hold of it. "I want you to meet my parents."

"Your parents?"

I saw Breeze raise one perfectly shaped eyebrow.

"I've told them all about you. Come on."

He's as good at this game as Breeze, I thought, pulling my hand away. When he reached back again, I stuffed both of them in my pockets. "I'm following," I assured him. As we passed a sofa, Gabriel and Jenny looked up at me and smiled.

"Hey, bro!" Jared greeted a tall guy who stood at the bottom of the basement stairs, leaning against the banister, talking to Kathleen. Leading me up the steps, Jared explained, "That's my older brother, Alex. He's a sophomore at Georgetown—got more brains than muscles."

Lucky for Kathleen, I thought. Aloud I said, "Why do your parents want to meet me?"

"They love your photos of me," he said, "the one you just gave me and other ones that have been in the newspaper."

Okay, I thought, *that makes sense*. But still, the arm around the waist and the hand-holding—nothing but the hope of getting to Breeze could account for that. As we entered the kitchen, three sets of football parents turned around to see who the nice girl was that

123

Jared was steering by the elbow.

"Mom, Dad, this is Hayley."

"Haaay-ley!" Mr. Wright greeted me just the way Jared did, which made me smile.

"Hayley Caldwell. We'd know that photo credit anywhere," said Mrs. Wright, opening her arms and giving me a bear hug. There was no question about where Jared and his older brother got their size—from *both* parents.

"Oh," said another parent, "are you the team photographer?"

I enjoyed the attention and compliments that followed. And I was a little surprised that Jared didn't try to slip away, but stood right next to me, beaming.

"You ought to show her our sports collection," Mr. Wright suggested to his son. Jared deftly caught hold of my hand again and led me on, and this time, I let him.

"This is my dad's office," he said, opening the door to a room with a desk, computer equipment, sofa, and bookcases. "He has always kept our good books in here, because my brothers and I pretty much destroyed anything left in the family room or the rec room downstairs."

I laughed. "How many brothers do you have?"

"Three. Two are married now. No sisters."

"Your poor mom!"

"Hey," he said, pointing to an old photo of a girl athlete

in a field hockey kilt, "she's the rowdiest of us all!"

I laughed again.

"I like the way you laugh, Hayley," Jared said, which immediately made me stop. He sounded a little too sincere.

I walked over to a built-in bookcase that covered an entire wall. One half of it was a shrine to Jared. He hadn't been kidding when he said his mother and grandmother kept scrapbooks. There were at least a dozen fat ones, perhaps one for each year since T-ball. I saw that I had made a decent contribution to the altar of photographs, not just his recent request, but laminated and framed sports pages that included the work of Gabriel and me. There were enough trophies to melt down steel for an SUV.

The other side of the bookcase was crammed with books about sports—historic teams, Baltimore's teams, famous players—books that had wonderful photos.

"Can I look through some of these?" I asked.

"My scrapbooks?" he replied hopefully, even though I was standing in front of the other books.

"Actually, I wanted to check out the historic photos," I said, hoping not to hurt his feelings, and also hoping to avoid a long tour through his life, which was sure to come with the scrapbooks.

"Okay," he said, and I chose several books from the shelf.

"Listen, Jared, this is your party," I told him as I carried the books to the sofa. "You're supposed to talk to everyone, so go ahead. I'd just like to look at these photographs for a few minutes—see how the pros do it."

"Me too," he replied. He sat down next to me, his leg against my leg. Of course, that made it easier if you were going to share a book.

We looked at a history of the Baltimore Colts before the team moved to Indianapolis—wonderful stuff, if you're a photo-freak like me. "I really love black and white photography."

"Me too," Jared said, stretching, then casually resting his arm along the back of the sofa, and just as casually letting it fall around my shoulders.

I stared at a great photo of Johnny Unitas, but I had lost my focus. All I could think of was how it had felt when I sat with Flynn and his little sisters, and Flynn's hand had rested on my shoulder. And while I was comparing the tingling I felt then to the absolute nothing that I felt now, I noticed that the party was downstairs, that Jared's parents were occupied in the kitchen, and that, while I was surveying the books, Jared had somehow managed to close the office door. Here I was alone on the sofa with the school's stud quarterback. Where was my sister when I needed her?

"Oh, I'm sorry," Breeze said, pushing open the door and taking a long look in.

Thank you, big sister! I thought. And then I thought, *Jared counted on this—he knew she'd follow to see what he was up to.* I didn't care—I was so glad for the interruption. "Breeze! Com'ere. Look at these books."

She entered the room, and to my surprise, so did Mike, the team's talented field goal kicker, a quirky guy who was the main baseball hero in the spring. Where was Flynn?

"Mike, would you look at all these books," Breeze said to him in a sweet, I'm-talking-to-you-only voice. I knew that voice, and I frowned. What was Breeze up to? Getting back at Jared? Keeping Flynn's attention? Moving on to Mike?

Jared and I moved over, allowing Breeze and Mike to join us on the sofa. It was all a little too cozy for me. A few minutes later, Jared's brother, Alex, came into the room with Kathleen, and they were followed by Flynn and a linebacker named Reggie and two cheerleaders.

Flynn's eyes surveyed the sofa sitters—Jared, me, Breeze, and Mike. Once again, I couldn't read the expression on his face. As for Reggie, he was only interested in finding a sandwich tray, and there were none in the office. But the cheerleaders were more observant. When the room began to feel unbearably warm and I excused myself, I heard one cheerleader say to the other, "Looks like both Caldwell girls made it into the starting lineup!"

11

On Saturday afternoon it became clear what Breeze was up to. Answering a knock at the door, I found Flynn, who was under the impression that he had a date with my sister. But, no, he had been stood up! Breeze did this whenever she felt that her boyfriend was taking her for granted. Most likely, Flynn had spent too much time talking to his teammates at last night's party, and this and the Mike-thing were a result. I told him exactly what she had told me: She'd be out all afternoon with a friend.

Perhaps it was the first time Flynn had been stood up by a girl. He stood quietly for a moment, thinking, then asked, "May I come in and wait?"

"For what?"

He laughed uncomfortably. "Maybe . . . she'll remember."

I looked at him as if he was extremely dense, and got the same look thrown back at me.

"Well, if that's what you want," I said, stepping back to let him in. Flynn glanced around, then sat down in front of the televised college game, which I had turned on while I was waiting for Gabriel to arrive. Once a month, Gabriel and I went bowling, and I was never so glad as today. *He'll be here any minute*, I told myself. In the meantime, I mentally drew a wide white border, then a thick wooden frame around my sister's boyfriend.

"So," Flynn said to me, "did you have a good time last night?"

"I always have a good time when we play well. And with so much scoring in the game, I have lots of decent photos to choose from. Actually, I have some excellent pictures of the defense, shots that show them being effective, which isn't as easy as showcasing the offense."

Flynn laughed. "I meant at the party, Hayley."

I knew what he had meant. And I knew Flynn was no dummy—he must have realized that Jared was trying to make Breeze jealous. He must have known that

I was being used in that cozy little sofa scene. Did he know that, when Jared rested his hand on my shoulder, I felt nothing, but when *he* touched me, I went electric? I hoped not.

"Oh, yeah," I said, "the party was nice."

The doorbell rang. Breathing a sigh of relief, I went to answer it.

"Jared!" I exclaimed.

"Hi, Hayley," he said, smiling.

"Hi. Uh, Breeze is out with a friend. She'll be gone all afternoon."

"Great!" he replied, and stepped inside the door. "Hey, you got the game on. Just like old times," he added, and started toward the family room. At the doorway he pulled up short. "Flynn."

"Jared. What are you doing here?"

"Visiting. How about you?"

"I'm . . . I'm waiting for Breeze."

Jared smiled and shook his head. "She's going to be out all afternoon."

"Yeah, that's what Hayley said," Flynn replied, glancing at me. "I thought she—she might remember and come back."

Jared laughed. "She won't. Trust me, old buddy, you've been stood up. You may as well go home."

"I see." Flynn's voice sounded tight.

"It's nothing to worry about," Jared added. "It's how Breeze dates."

Flynn nodded. "Well, it's not like we're going steady."

"Actually, with Breeze, it's how she dates even when you're going steady."

There was a sharp rap on the frame of the front door. "Just me, Hay," a deep voice called through the screen.

"Now who is it?" Flynn asked.

"Come on in, Gabriel," I called.

"Hey, guys," Gabriel said as he entered the room. "Good party last night, Jared. Ready to go, Hayley?"

"Let me grab my purse." I turned to Flynn and Jared. "If you guys want to hang out together and watch the game, that's fine with me. There's soda in the fridge."

"You're going out? Now?" Jared asked, as if it had never occurred to him that I might not want to hang around with him, that I might have made some Saturday plans of my own. "Where are you going?"

"Bowling."

He and Flynn exchanged glances. Of course, bowling's not considered one of the cooler sports, not once you get out of elementary school.

"Ten pins?" Jared asked.

"Duckpins," I replied. "A game of skill."

"I haven't rolled duckpins since third grade," Flynn remarked.

"Me neither," Jared said. "Can I come—old buddy?"

I shook my head at Gabriel as subtly as possible, trying to signal him, but Jared had rested his heavy hand on Gabriel's shoulder, hoping for a return favor for last night's invite to the party.

"Sure," Gabriel replied. "That'd be fun."

"Can I come too?" Flynn asked.

Again, I shook my head.

"You mean with Breeze?" Gabriel asked back, frowning a little, and totally missing my signal to him.

"She's out all afternoon," Flynn said.

"Well, then, sure. Four will even it off."

Which is how I ended up spending Saturday afternoon with two hot jocks and one cute, sensitive-looking type. The girl at the bowling alley, who was handing out rental shoes, whispered to me, "Wow! What's your secret?"

I sighed. "A sister who plays too many games."

The three guys and I arrived back at my house at four thirty. Breeze must have gotten home just before that. Recognizing Flynn's Toyota parked in front of our house, she sat on the front porch, reading a magazine and waiting. The look of wonder on the bowling clerk's face was nothing compared to the look on Breeze's when the four of us climbed out of Jared's car.

"Hey, you're home," Flynn said to Breeze, smiling easily as he walked up the path.

I realized then that Breeze had met her match. This was not a guy who was going to mope around when stood up; he could always find something fun to do.

Apparently, Breeze realized this too. She treated him to a movie that evening—*not* a chick flick. Ten minutes after she arrived home from the film, she knocked on the bathroom door. "I'm home. I have a question, Hayley."

I opened the door, my mouth full of toothpaste foam.

"When you're done," Breeze said.

I shut it again, wishing I had gone to bed early. When I entered her bedroom she was sitting at her dressing table, contemplating her hairbrush. The little knit top she wore must have been new. She looked totally fantastic in it.

She turned to me. "Hayley, why did Jared come over today?"

"I don't know."

My sister studied me, her head cocked to one side.

"I really don't know. He just showed up."

She nodded slowly. "He's trying to win me back."

"Is that why you're dating Flynn?" I asked. "Are you trying to win back Jared?"

"That's why I was at first," she admitted. "Now . . ." She

shrugged, then laughed. "So many guys, so little time."

I winced. She saw it.

"Lighten up, Hayley," she said, leaning over so she could brush her hair up from the back of her neck.

"Don't you ever worry about hurting people?"

"People like who?"

"Flynn."

She pulled her head up quickly. Her hair flew back, shimmering in the lamplight.

"And Jared, and Mike," I added, but she had already heard the tone in my voice.

"*Oooh*. Do we just happen to have a teensy-weensy crush on Flynn?"

"We?" I repeated. "I can only speak for myself. And the answer is no."

"Well, *I* think that the answer may be—"

"No," I said firmly. It was the absolute truth. There was nothing at all *teensy-weensy* about my feelings for Flynn.

"So then, are you feeling sorry for him? Don't forget, Hayley, he pursued me first. He knows the game, all the risks and all the tricks. When it comes to dating, Flynn is varsity all-star."

I nodded. How could I forget any of that?

"You take everything so seriously," she said, laughing. Then she leaned close to her mirror and studied her chin. "God, I hope that's not a zit."

And I hoped fervently that it was a *hundred* zits; then I felt bad. For the first time in my life, I had let a guy come between my sister and me.

Breeze pulled back from the mirror and turned toward me. "It's funny, you know. Just when Jared shows up again, I realize how much I like Flynn."

"Funny."

"The fall dance is next week. I guess you're covering it for the paper."

"Yeah," I said, and headed back to my bedroom.

"Jared and Mike can only stay for an hour, you know, with Siefert's stupid curfew."

I closed the door softly. "I know. G'night."

"Fortunately, Flynn can be out with me forever and ever."

With her forever and ever. I climbed in bed and clicked off my lamp.

"Flynn is so gorgeous!" Breeze went on. "And smart. And cool."

I wanted to pull the pillow over my head.

"And classy. And sort of rich. And—Hayley?"

I *did* pull the pillow over my head.

"Am I talking to myself?" she asked.

"Yes," I called back. "G'night."

12

*S*unday afternoon, a voice as light as a fairy's said
on the phone, "Hi, Hayley. Can you come over?"

"Emma?"

"We got the kitten. Can you come over? Would you
bring your camera?"

"My turn!" I heard. "Gimme, Emma!"

"No, I'm talking!"

"My turn! My turn!"

"Meggieeeeee!" That was followed by a howl.

"Emma scratched me!" A second howl joined the first.

"Hello?" I said. "Hello . . ."

"Hi," said Flynn.

"Hi."

Oh, great, I thought, *all he did was say hello and my cheeks are hot.*

"We got the kitten."

"So I heard."

"I'm babysitting," he continued.

"And you have everything under control, I can tell."

He laughed. "If you would like to come over, they could fight over you as well as the kitten, and poor Fang might survive."

"Fang—sweet name."

"I like it."

There was a long moment of silence.

"So do you want to come over?" he asked. "The girls and I can pick you up and—"

Breeze's voice came from behind me. "I'll take it now," she said. "I saw the caller ID."

"Breeze is right here," I told Flynn, "asking to talk to you."

"Hayley? Hayley, I—"

Breeze pulled the phone out of my hands. "Hi. What's going on?" she asked, then frowned a little. "Babysitting? Well, if Hayley wants to come, I could drive her over. Let me see what she's doing." Breeze punched mute. "Do you want to go see a kitten?"

"Sure." I didn't want to disappoint Meg and Emma, and if Breeze was there, I wouldn't have to worry about being alone with Flynn.

Breeze pressed the mute button. "We'll be there soon."

That meant an hour. By the time we got to the Delancys' home, the girls were wild with waiting. They grabbed my hands and led me to the kitchen, where the kitten was being kept until it became used to the house.

The little tabby was very sweet, and probably should have been called Fluffy rather than Fang. Breeze and I petted him. Then the girls wanted to take him outside for his photo shoot. They put a pink harness on him and attached a long string to that, since their yard wasn't completely fenced in. They loved fussing over him. I figured it wouldn't be long before Fang found himself dressed up in more than a harness.

Meg carried the kitten out to the patio, followed by Emma and her Barbie camera, and me and my digital.

"I would love something to drink, Flynn," I heard Breeze say as we exited, and I knew the two of them would stay inside.

Emma and I took several pictures of Fang on the stone patio.

"Let me take some shots of you holding him," I said

to the girls, surveying the Delancys' large yard. The light on the shaded patio was too blue, but I knew the bright sun would make the girls squint. About seventy-five feet away was an old maple that had dropped many of its leaves early, making it a soft filter for the sun. I pointed to it. "Over there."

With three adorable subjects, I was sure to get some good pictures, but the constant movement made them as challenging as a football team. The girls wanted to teach Fang tricks, and the kitten was very glad to chase a piece of string. The problem was, he was also glad to chase leaves, pieces of grass, a moving hand, and his own tail.

When Fang discovered a strand of my hair that had fallen from my clip, the girls thought it was funny. Emma pulled out the clip and my ponytail tumbled down. The girls shrieked with laughter as Fang attacked and batted and chewed. I handed him to Emma so I could gather up my hair, but Emma let go of the kitten, just as a squirrel ran by. Fang took off, and in a flash he was up the tree. He didn't stop climbing until he was *way* up.

The girls and I jumped to our feet and rushed to the base of the maple. The old tree had a million branches going in different directions, making it very easy for a little cat to climb. The not-so-easy part would be getting down.

"Here, Fang. Here, kitty, kitty."

At first the kitten paid no attention to us. He was fascinated by the birds that flew at the same height as he. But after a few minutes, perhaps when it became clear that the squirrel had escaped and the birds did not wish to be his friends, the kitten looked down at us, his round face grave.

"Here, Fang. Here, kitty kitty."

Fang eased a paw down, got nervous, and pulled it back. He did this for about two minutes, then he started to cry, which made Emma and Meg cry.

"He's fine," I said. "He's fine. He's a little scared, that's all."

Just as I said that, Fang tried again, but this time his paws slipped and he dropped six inches. Part of his string got hooked on a branch. *Oh, God*, I thought, *he's going to hang himself.* "Go get Flynn," I told them, trying to keep my voice calm. Grabbing hold of the lowest branch, I started climbing.

Meg ran to the house, screaming. Emma stayed beneath the tree, sobbing.

"Everything's going to be all right, Emma."

I hadn't gotten very far when I discovered there was a reason that the tree had lost many of its leaves early—parts of it were rotten. I had to feel my way onto each branch, testing before putting my weight on it. Several branches cracked ominously.

I was a good twenty feet up, but still several feet below the cat, when I heard the back door of the house slam.

Meg ran toward us, screaming and pointing up at me. I saw Flynn standing on the patio for a moment, as if puzzled, then he realized it was me in the tree and came running.

"What are you doing up there?" he shouted.

"Catching squirrels."

Reaching the base, he stopped and peered up at me. "Oh, jeez. Why didn't you call me? You should have called me as soon as the cat started up."

"So you could climb the tree one-armed?"

"Hayley, this maple is half-rotten. We've been waiting for the tree service to come take it down."

"Well, when I'm done, you may not need them," I said. I slid my foot up the trunk, tested a branch that cracked loudly, then tried another. I was scared, but I knew I couldn't stand watching a kitten hang itself. Finally, Fang was within reach. Stretching up my hand, I unhooked him from his tangled leash, then grabbed hold of him.

Terrified, the kitten sank his little needle claws into my arm. I pulled him down and held him against my chest, talking to him, trying to soothe him. Gripping the ball of fur with one hand and the tree trunk with the other, I slowly made my descent.

"Be careful," Flynn pleaded.

I was about twelve feet from the ground when Fang realized he was close, close for a cat, I guess. Wrenching himself free, he scrambled onto a side branch, but missed his footing. For a moment he hung from his front paws, then he dropped, twisting his body in midair, landing neatly on all fours. Proud of himself, the kitten raced off. The girls shouted and ran after him.

Flynn stayed beneath the tree. "Please be careful, Hayley," he said, his face turned up to me.

"Listen, I've climbed a forest of trees in my—" *Crrrack!*

One moment I was glancing down at Flynn. The next, a blur of leaves flew by and the ground rushed up to meet me. My fall ended with a loud *thlump.* I lay there stunned, aware of tree branches and leaves in a pile around me.

"Are you okay? Hayley, are you okay?"

Flynn's voice was muffled, coming from beneath me—he had cushioned my fall.

"Oh! Oh my gosh!" I said, trying to pull myself up quickly and digging my elbow sharply into his ribs.

"Umph."

"Oh, sorry! I'm so sorry, I hope I didn't hurt you," I said, then pressed my knee into his abdomen.

"Agh."

"Oh, no!" I quickly rolled sideways and fell onto his arm, the broken one.

"Hayley!"

"Your arm! Oh, God, I've hurt your arm!"

"Hayley, stop!" His left hand held me still. "Don't move, just don't move until we can figure out where everything is."

I lay very still. I could hear Flynn's heart. I could feel his breathing. His hand relaxed against my back. The last time I had been this close to him, all I could think about was whether I had broken the school camera. Now all I could think about was Flynn.

Then he began to shake—he was laughing. I slid off him and we both sat up.

"Well, now I've got a bruise on my butt that's going to look like a bouquet of pansies," he said, "which makes us even." He reached out and pulled a twig from my hair. "You're sure you're okay?" he asked, still laughing, reaching to brush a tumble of hair out of my face.

Suddenly he stopped. Just . . . stopped.

I met his eyes. They were autumn blue, as full of light as the sky. I knew I should look away—I knew my eyes would tell him secrets he wasn't supposed to know, but I kept looking. His hand stayed where it was, half touching my cheek.

I saw Flynn swallow hard. With one finger, he softly touched my lips. He pulled his hand back a little. He swallowed again. With a single finger, touching me ever so lightly, he traced my mouth. His face drew closer and closer to mine.

"We've got him!" Meg cried. "We've got him."

Flynn and I pulled back, and the girls belly flopped on top of us.

"Everybody jump in the leaves!" Emma said, throwing handfuls of them in the air. The kitten climbed around, enjoying the landscape of collapsed bodies and tree branches.

"What's going on out there?" Breeze called. Turning my head, I saw that she was standing on the patio, but I didn't know how long she had been there.

I struggled to my feet. "Fang got stuck in the tree. I got him unstuck—not very gracefully," I added.

Flynn rose and brushed himself off. I walked over to where I had left my camera and hair clip. Not wanting to meet his eyes again, definitely not wanting to look at my sister, I did the only thing that could make me feel half-way normal. I started reviewing the photos I had taken. But I wasn't really looking at the digital images. All I was seeing were Flynn's eyes. All I was feeling was the light touch of his finger on my lips.

"Keep Fang away from the tree, girls," Flynn told his sisters. When I glanced over at them, half of Flynn's mouth drew up in a wry smile. "Better keep Hayley away from it, too," he added, then started toward the patio. Flynn and Breeze went back inside.

Emma and Meg told Fang how naughty he was, then Meg said, "I'm thirsty."

"Me, too," said Emma.

"Let's get some juice. Hayley?"

"Huh? Oh. Okay." I followed the girls and Fang.

When we entered the house I was relieved to find the kitchen empty and the two doors leading to the rest of the house closed. I felt strange—almost shaky. My fingers wouldn't work right. Emma looked at me curiously when I sloshed the juice in her cup.

The girls and I were sipping our drinks, with the exhausted Fang lying on my foot, when I heard footsteps enter the room next to us.

"So," Breeze said, her voice carrying, "are we dating?"

"What do you mean?" Flynn replied.

Meg and Emma turned their heads, looking at the door to the family room.

"Are you dating me or not?" Breeze demanded.

"Isn't it obvious?" Flynn asked.

"It's obvious to me that you like to play around!"

There was a long silence, and Meg asked softly, "What does 'play around' mean?"

Before I could think of a good answer, Flynn's voice broke in. "I'm not blind, Breeze. You play around even more than me!"

"Not under a tree, I don't!"

My hand gripped my cup.

I could hear someone walking back and forth—Flynn pacing.

"You play the game well, Breeze," he said, "but it doesn't take much to get you worried."

Get her worried? Was that the plan?

"What I'm worried about," Breeze replied, "is who you're playing around with. She's very innocent, Flynn, very naïve and vulnerable. I don't want to see her heart broken. Do you understand?"

I understood. My cheeks flamed.

"I think," Emma said to Meg, "*playing around* means playing outside."

"Let's go outside now," I told the girls.

"Flynn!" Meg called. "What does *playing around* mean?"

There was a long and awful silence. Then footsteps sounded and the door between the kitchen and family room opened. Breeze sat on the leather sofa. Flynn, filling the doorframe, looked in at us, first at the girls, then me. I forced myself to look back. His mouth was a straight line, his eyes hooded. I knew my cheeks were beet red. Turning away, I gathered the juice cups, and put them in the sink. "Emma thought it meant playing outside," I said.

I heard Flynn take a deep breath and let it out slowly. "It means playing outside the lines, Emma."

"Like out-of-bounds?"

"Like out-of-bounds," he replied quietly.

I picked up the kitten. "Fang and I are going back to the garden. Want to come, girls?"

I left without waiting for an answer.

13

For the next three days I kept a low profile, my face in a textbook, behind my camera, or glued to a computer screen. I figured that if I could jam enough words and images in my brain, there wouldn't any room left for Flynn. I avoided Breeze. I avoided lunch in the cafeteria and passing anywhere near Breeze's locker and the football stadium. I didn't answer the phone.

Wednesday, we put the paper to bed at four o'clock, as usual. Jenny got picked up by her mother soon after, to see a film in D.C. with her mother's class. Paige had an appointment for a haircut. Dillon and the others drifted away, until it was just Kathleen, Gabriel, and me.

Gabriel typed rapidly in the corner of the newspaper

office. Kathleen sat down on a chair near to me, wheeling it closer.

"How's everything?" she asked.

I kept my eyes on the photos of the drama group laid out on the screen in front of me.

"Good."

"You've been quiet," she said.

"Well, I've had a lot to work on."

"You always have a lot to work on, Hayley, but there's a kind of happiness in the way you bounce from one thing to another. And that's missing."

I stared down at my keyboard. "It'll come back," I said. "I just need to lie low for a while until—" I shrugged, because it felt like my feelings for Flynn would never end. "Until I don't need to lie low anymore."

She nodded. "Okay. You know I'm glad to listen. You have my cell number," she said, and left.

I will get through this, I told myself, and worked hard on the drama club's rehearsal photos, pausing for only a moment to study Nicole, Flynn's old girlfriend, flirting with the camera. Fake, but very beautiful. *Fool!* I told her, and moved on.

"You're muttering to yourself, Hayley," Gabriel said.

"This is a democracy, I have a right."

He laughed and came over, taking the chair that Kathleen had vacated. "Can we talk?"

Oh, no, not more questions. "Depends. What's the subject?"

"Jenny."

I stopped working on the photos in front of me. "Okay."

"I'm trying to decide whether I should ask her to the fall formal."

"And you're asking *me* for advice? Gabriel, you know I am as dumb about guy-and-girl stuff as you are." I thought for a moment. "Dumber, actually."

"But you're a girl," he said. "And I'm a guy. So between us we should be able to figure it out."

I laughed. I hadn't laughed for three days and it felt good.

"I guess so," I agreed. "So what's the problem? Do you want to take her?"

"Oh, yeah!"

"So then, why wouldn't you ask her?"

"I'm afraid I'll scare her away."

I slid my mouse back and forth, making the arrow jump all over the screen. "When you're around her, when it's just you and her, does she sometimes act like she's pulling away?"

"No. No, it's just that—" He ran a hand through his curly hair.

"Just that?"

"I really like her, Hayley. I mean, I really, really like her. Really."

"*Really*," I said, laughing, but I could feel the tears behind my eyes. He was so sincere. His feelings were closer to true love than any of those jocks with their tons of experience at playing around. "Then I think you have to take the chance."

"But here's the thing," he said. "I'd rather be around her as just a friend than not at all. And if I scare her off—"

"I think that if you scare off Jenny, she will get over it. Maybe not as soon as you'd like, but she will eventually. And all the time, I'll be here as your friend."

Gabriel looked at me, then smiled, his eyes warm and brown. "I know you will, Hayley. Thanks!" He gave me a quick shy hug, then stood up.

"You better ask her fast. It's already Wednesday and people wear fancy clothes."

He nodded. "You walking home?"

"Yeah, but go ahead. I have a lot more I want to do."

"I'll lock the door behind me," he said, then gathered his stuff and left.

As soon as the door clicked shut, I pressed my hands against my face. One tear rolled down—only one, and that was mostly because, in squeezing my eyes tight, one of the tears went the wrong way. I was *not* going to cry.

For the next twenty minutes I worked on drama pictures, then I went to my locker, got chewed out by a teacher who reminded me that students weren't supposed to be in the building that late, and left. The football team must have still been practicing because there were cars in the student parking lot. I walked quickly.

A storm was brewing. The wind had picked up and a mass of purple clouds was coming in from the west. It felt good to have my hair whipping around my head. I thought it might feel good to have hail beat down on me. Sometimes storms outside are the only relief for storms inside.

"Hayley. Hayley! *Earth to Hayley!*"

I stopped between a maroon SUV and a lime-colored sports car. "Flynn."

He started to walk around the car, then stopped, as if he sensed me pulling back and knew I wanted that car to stay between us. He studied me a moment.

"How are you?" he asked.

"Fine. How's Fang?"

"Growing. We've kept him out of the tree—so far."

"Good."

"Hayley, listen, I—"

"You've got a new cast," I interrupted. The way he had

153

just said my name, gently, like a guy who knew he was talking to a girl who was innocent, vulnerable, ridiculously naïve—like a guy who was going to apologize for the best moment of my life! I couldn't stand it. "The cast looks more comfortable," I said.

"It's much smaller," he replied. "I can get it through a sleeve."

"Good."

"Hayley, I haven't seen you for several days."

He paused, as if hoping I'd offer an explanation. I just stood there, letting my hair fly around.

"I guess you were out last night when I came over."

"Yes."

"And the night before?"

"Yes."

"Are you going home now?"

"Yes."

"Can I give you a ride?"

"No."

The word hung in the air between us, big as a highway sign, one that said EXIT ONLY. "I, uh, like walking," I added, trying not to sound so stiff.

"But it's going to storm," he pointed out.

"I like storming, too."

"I see."

"Bye." I walked on quickly and was glad to hear someone

calling Flynn's name, so I didn't have to feel his eyes on my back.

I had just reached the end of the school driveway when a red Hyundai pulled up next to me. The driver's window slid down. "Haaay-ley. My favorite photographer!"

I don't need this right now! I thought, but aloud I said, "Hi, Jared."

"Have you been working on the newspaper?" he asked. "How's the sports page looking?"

"Good."

"It's coming out Friday?"

"Yes."

"Can't wait to see it!"

And laminate it and frame it, I thought.

"I just came from football practice."

"Good."

"It was great. Coach seemed really pleased today."

"Glad to hear it."

"I think we're finally putting the pieces together."

"Great."

"Hey, how about a ride home?" he asked. "Your hair's looking like a tornado," he added with a grin.

The wind was really whipping up. I felt the first fat raindrop splash on my arm. It would be a long, wet walk home.

"Actually, that would be nice."

Jared yanked on the emergency brake, leaped out of his car rather dramatically, took the stack of books from my hands, and carried them around to the other side. I followed. I heard a car drive up behind Jared's. Jared waved it around, then leaned down to "help" me with my seatbelt.

"Thanks, I've got it."

He closed the door and strode around to his side, waving again to the car behind him. As he buckled his seatbelt, he started telling me about practice, going into details that only Coach—or maybe his mother and grandmother—would want to hear. The driver behind us finally gave up. As the car pulled around to the right, I glanced over and saw Flynn fling a glance in our direction.

Jared talked all the way home, then sat in the car in front of my house and talked some more. When he took a breath, I reached for the door handle.

"Hayley, wait," he said. "I have something to ask you. Would you go to the dance?"

"Would I—What?"

"Go to the dance."

"With *you*?"

"Of course, I can only take you for the first hour. You know Coach's rules. But I was thinking that might be perfect. We could go together, and then after I left, you could stay and take pictures."

I sat back in the seat. Amazingly, his idea made some sense. He could go to the dance with a date. I could wear the dress I had been saving for a special occasion. Then he could leave without angering his date, and I was free to take pictures.

Was this another attempt to get to Breeze? Or was he simply maintaining his pride by taking a date to the dance, a girl who'd be willing to accompany him for an hour and expect nothing more? I decided I didn't care. It helped him and it helped me, and we weren't misleading each other. We weren't hurting anyone.

"I was thinking I could take you out to dinner first," he said. "We could go to the harbor."

"Oh, you don't have to do that," I told him.

"But I'd like to," he said. "I love eating out."

I shrugged. "Well . . . okay. Okay!"

That evening, when Breeze needed to borrow paper, she saw my long dress hanging on the hook inside my closet door. She lifted down the hanger and held the gown up to herself, gazing in the mirror.

The dress was a dark satiny rose, with a full skirt and little spaghetti straps that left my shoulders and much of my back bare. I had fallen in love with it during the after-prom sales of last year and had bought it in one of my weak moments with Breeze, telling myself that eventually, whenever I got to wear it, it would be a bargain.

"Red would be more striking," she said.

"But this is the color I love," I replied.

"What shoes are you going to wear?" She hung up the dress, and started foraging in my closet.

"I don't know. Until now, I hadn't planned to dress up for the dance."

She was off in a flash. I heard a landslide of boxes in her closet, then she returned carrying an incredible pair of tall, curvy, silver shoes.

"Wow. Have I seen those before?"

"Probably not. They never went with anything I had. Try them on, try them on."

I kicked off my slides. Princess shoes! My feet looked fabulous in them.

"The dress, too, silly!"

As I pulled it on, I listened to her rummaging through the bathroom vanity. She brought back three polishes and held them against the dress. "This one, I think, Sunset Rose," she said, "although you should try all of them to be sure. Color can be so deceiving. Different brands of polish reflect back light in different ways."

She was putting me together as carefully as I composed a photograph.

"What are you going to do with your hair?" she asked.

"I don't know."

"An updo with some long pieces," she said, placing the nail polishes on my desk. "And, I think—yes—little roses. Too sweet for me, but right for you. I wonder how hard it would be to get roses that match your dress. . . . No, no, *white* ones!" She started lifting my hair in hunks, holding it above my head. "Pure white ones that will make your hair look dark and rich. Perfect!"

She dropped my hair and stepped back. "I think you should get your hair done professionally. It's been my experience that getting it to stay up—and getting stuff to stay in it—never really works when you do it yourself."

"Isn't that expensive?"

"You get what you pay for, Hayley," she said. "It wouldn't hurt if just once everyone at school sees what you look like at your best."

"And I can wear these shoes?"

"You *must* wear them," she said, "though they'll make you taller than Gabriel," she added with a slight frown. "Well, that's his problem."

"I think Gabriel is going with Jenny."

"Gabriel and Jenny? What are *you* going to do?"

"I'm going with Jared."

Her eyes opened wide. For a moment, I was afraid the magic shoes were going to disappear, then she sat on my bed looking thoughtful.

"Of course, you will be going for only an hour," she said.

"That's right. It works out great. When he goes home, I'll take pictures. But we're going to the harbor for dinner first." I just had to add that.

She nodded as if she understood. "Probably Phillips. He loves Phillips's food."

"So do I."

She contemplated her nails, wiggled her fingers, then dropped her hands in her lap. "Be careful, Hayley."

I stepped out of the wonderful shoes. "Careful of what?"

"Hayley, you must see what Jared is doing! It's obvious. He's using you to get to me."

"Don't worry. It's just that Jared and I both need a date. And I don't mind listening to football stuff, and—"

"Are you saying I never listened to him? Are you saying I never enjoyed eating at Phillips, even if it is a noisy crab house and totally unromantic?"

She seemed a little sensitive at the moment. "Listen to me, Breeze. This is one of those arrangements that works conveniently for both of us. It doesn't mean Jared and I are hot for each other—we're definitely not."

"Mmm," was all she said.

As she walked out of the room, I asked, "Where should I get my hair done?"

She shrugged. "Every place I know is expensive."

14

$\mathscr{F}$riday evening, like a well-coached player, I kept my eyes on the field for every second of play. During time-outs when the players were on the sidelines, I reviewed my pictures, avoiding even a glimpse of Flynn. At halftime, Meg, Emma, and Dr. Delancy caught me at the hot dog stand.

Jared had sent a message by way of Gabriel before the game, saying we were all invited to the football party, which was being held at Mike's house. After the game, I met Jared in the parking lot and told him I was too tired to go.

He rested a heavy hand on my shoulder. "I'm beat, too.

Let's go home to your house and watch TV."

So you can be there when Breeze comes home? I wondered. Of course, it was possible that he really was exhausted, but I'd done enough sofa-sitting with him.

"I don't think that's a good idea, Jared."

"You don't?"

"The party's a team thing, and you're the team leader. You should be there."

He considered my argument.

"Even if it's just for a short time, you should be there for the guys. And if you go home early, that's okay. It will set a good example."

He smiled. "You give good advice, Hayley."

I shrugged.

"You're always looking out for me. You're always thinking about what's good for me as a player." There was an odd kind of warmth in Jared's voice. "You're my best fan!" He gave me a bone-crunching hug, lifting me right off my feet.

When he moved on, I saw several team members looking in our direction. I glanced away from them, and my eyes ran into Flynn's, observing me over my sister's shoulder.

Kathleen dropped me off at home, then she, Gabriel, and Jenny went on to the party. From the smile on Gabriel's face, I figured he had a date for tomorrow night's dance.

♡ ♡

Saturday at five thirty P.M., the doorbell rang.

"I'll get it for you, honey," my father said, putting down his magazine.

"Thanks." I opened my camera bag on a family room table to make sure I had extra batteries and memory sticks.

"Hi, Jared," I called without turning around. "I'm just packing up. At least I don't have to worry about anything getting wet. It's an absolutely perfect night."

"Yes. It is."

At the sound of Flynn's voice, I straightened up. Why did he always come so early? He just couldn't seem to catch on to Breeze's schedule. He made me crazy!

I forced myself to turn around slowly, as I would have for Jared. In his dark suit, Flynn looked five years older and absolutely gorgeous. Neither of us could think of anything to say. Staring at each other, we stood as still as mannequins in a shop window. Maybe it was the high heels, but I felt dizzy.

"I'm sorry, Jared," my father said, breaking the spell. "I was sure you were Flynn."

"He is, Dad. My mistake."

"There's just so many of you," my father continued apologetically.

Flynn laughed dryly. "I understand, Mr. Caldwell. This

place is a regular landing strip for guys."

"More and more," my father said, then returned to his chair and hid behind his magazine.

"You're here really early for Breeze, you know."

"I know," Flynn replied.

I picked up the TV remote and held it out to him.

He didn't take it right away. "You look . . . good, Hayley."

"Thank you." The doorbell rang again. "I'll get it, Dad."

I opened the door and let in another great-looking guy in a suit.

"Wow!" Jared exclaimed. "Wow! Haaay-leeeeey!"

I laughed. Jared's reaction was kind of overdone and loud, but he meant to be nice, and I was in desperate need of some compliments and encouragement. "Come on in while I get my camera bag and purse. Oh, and my running shoes. After you leave the dance I'm going to prowl around in something other than these," I told him, lifting my skirt so he could see.

He whistled appreciatively, and I laughed again, then led him into the family room.

"I like the roses in your hair," he said.

"Thanks!" I was grateful to him for noticing—the salon had definitely set me back on my camera fund.

"Hey, Mr. Caldwell. Hey, Flynn."

Both Dad and Flynn stood up. Dad shook hands, then withdrew to his magazine.

"Doesn't Hayley look incredible?" Jared said to Flynn.

"Yes."

"Looks a whole lot different from when she's taking pictures on the sideline, huh?"

Flynn nodded, but said nothing. I felt my cheeks getting warm.

"Remember when Flynn ran over you in preseason," Jared said to me, "and he never even noticed?"

Flynn tilted his head back slightly, the kind of gesture that could quickly turn into a scowl.

"Well, if you'd looked like this," Jared added enthusiastically, "I guarantee you, he would've noticed."

"Not necessarily," Flynn said.

My cheeks went from warm to flaming hot.

"When I'm focused on football, all I see is football. It doesn't matter who else is there—or what she looks like."

"Jared, I'm getting hungry. Let's go."

"Whatever you say, beautiful!"

I carried my running shoes and fancy beaded purse—Breeze's beaded purse—and didn't argue when Jared insisted on carrying my camera bag to his car.

By the time we were parked in a downtown garage

next to Harborplace, it had become clear that Jared was enjoying an enthusiastic and loud night. So I guessed it was lucky that we were eating at a touristy place, rather than in a restaurant with romantic candlelight and white tablecloths. Families, couples, and groups of people with visitor tags from a convention were lined up outside the door of Phillips.

We decided to wait for a table on the outdoor patio. With Jared's name on the list at the front desk and a forty-five–minute wait, we walked the wide brick promenade that ran along the harbor, pausing to sit on a bench now and then. We talked football, and football, and football—NFL, college, high school—Jared doing a lot of the talking.

As we walked, I gazed out at the water, its silky purple surface beginning to speckle with lights from small pleasure boats. A large Brazilian ship was docked along one side of the harbor; the sailors looked down at us and waved. A water taxi sounded its horn and slid away from its pier. Rising behind the restaurants and little shops, skyscrapers made tall patterns of light. Only three times—okay, four, maybe five—did I wonder what it would be like to walk in such a romantic place with Flynn.

When we arrived back at the restaurant, we had to wait five more minutes but were given a fabulous table at the far end of the patio. Large concrete containers overflowing with flowers separated us from the people walking the promenade. For a few minutes I watched the people and the boats beyond them. I didn't need to look at the menu; I always ordered the same thing.

"I always get the same thing," Jared said, and I laughed. He turned to see if there was a waiter in sight. "Hey, look who's here."

I knew before I looked, and I guessed that it had been Breeze's idea. Forty feet away, she and Flynn were being seated. She just had to come, too, even if it was "totally unromantic."

Earlier in the day, I had seen her black dress lying on the bed, but I hadn't seen it *on* her. Yes, I did look "good," maybe even very pretty, but if Breeze had walked by that Brazilian boat, the crew would have abandoned ship. I turned to see Jared's reaction to my sister. He quickly, somewhat guiltily, shifted his eyes back to me. "Best place in town to eat," he said, then went on to discuss food with almost as much enthusiasm as football.

We gave our orders and the crab soup came immediately. When we were nearly through spooning up the delicious stuff, Jared said in a voice that was unusually serious for him, "Hayley, you're so good for me."

I smiled uneasily. *What did that mean?*

"I'm so glad I found you."

"Excuse me?"

"It's so funny," he said. "I really thought I wanted Breeze."

I set down my spoon.

"You're both great," Jared continued, then stole a glance toward my sister. "I mean, she's gorgeous. . . She's *hot*!" He tore his eyes away from her. "But you're so much easier to be with."

Easier!

The waiter removed our soup bowls and brought our salads.

"You really understand me, Hayley," Jared went on. "You know football enough to fully appreciate my talent. You completely understand the stress I'm under. You do whatever you can to help me, and I *like* that."

He reached for my fingers, but I was too quick for him. He pulled back his throwing hand from the fork I now brandished.

"You put me first," he went on, "and not a lot of girls know how to do that."

I frowned, but he didn't seem to notice.

"*None* of the *pretty* ones," he added, shaking his head.

I stuck my fork into my salad, launching a cherry tomato.

"You're just terrific, Hayley! I—I think I'm falling in love with you!"

"But Jared—"

"You're the perfect girlfriend."

"Jared, I—"

"The perfect girl for an athlete like me."

"Jared—"

"With you, my parents, and Coach Siefert, how can I fail? This isn't just about tonight, Hayley. I want you with me every step of the way. I want you to be my girl."

"Jared!"

"What?"

"You forgot to ask what I want."

He was silent for a moment. "I just assumed."

"Exactly."

His face was a pumpkin-sized blank. "I don't understand."

"Listen," I said, "I had no idea you were thinking about me in this—this confused way. During the last few weeks, I thought you were paying attention to me because you were trying to get to Breeze."

"I was at first," he replied. "That's what's so funny. Flynn and I made an arrangement, because I thought I wanted Breeze, and then, all of a sudden, I realized *you* were the perfect girl!"

"Flynn and you—what arrangement?"

"Well, I knew Breeze was going to be impossible to manage during the football season. You know I've got to perform, Hayley. I've got to do what Siefert says. I've got to—"

"I know that part. Move on!"

"Everybody knows that if you don't pay enough attention to Breeze, she wanders. And there was no way I could pay enough attention to her during the season. So when Flynn got hurt, and Nicole dumped him, I asked him for a favor. I asked him to take one more hit for the team, if you know what I mean."

"Keep going," I said.

"It was simple. I pretended to want to break up with Breeze, and he pretended to want to date her."

"He's just pretending . . ."

"*Was*," Jared corrected me. "Was pretending. It was so easy. I mean, if anyone knows how to come on to a girl, Flynn does. Heck, if they offered college scholarships for *that*, Flynn would—"

"I get your point," I said.

"I just needed him to keep her occupied, and then, at the end of the season, he was going to break up with her, and I could have her back. But here's the funny thing," Jared went on. "Yesterday Flynn told me that he couldn't keep pretending like this."

"Because?"

"He's in love, poor guy! In love like I *never* was.

Everyone on the team has noticed it—I mean, Flynn's in another world. He has totally lost his focus. I've never seen a guy in so over his head! So I put him out of his misery. I told him he could have Breeze. Sure, she's hot." Jared glanced in her direction. "Incredibly hot," he felt compelled to add, "but she's way too much trouble."

I wanted to scream. I wanted to throw dishes. All this time, Flynn and Jared had been playing a game. Flynn had gotten burned by his own game and, given Breeze's flirty ways, he would continue to get burned. Meanwhile, he'd made me miserable, too. As for Jared, he was obviously in love with Breeze and wanted me to be a—a—a freaking football nanny!

I struggled to stay calm. "Did it ever occur to you, Jared, that love isn't easy? Did you ever stop to think that love, the real thing, could be more difficult to find—and keep—than anything else, including a football scholarship?"

"Not with someone like you," he said, reaching for my hand again.

I pulled back.

"You're such a sweet girl, Hayley."

"Sweet? Kind of innocent? Naïve?" I added, hating the description.

"Yeah! I don't know why I thought I'd never want to date a girl like you."

I stood up slowly. "I can't imagine either," I said. Then I picked up his salad, and dumped it on his head.

From the tables around us came a sharp intake of breath. Jared gazed up at me, speechless. I grabbed my purse and out of the corner of my eye saw Flynn and Breeze staring at us. Flynn started laughing.

I walked over to their table. Flynn was helpless with laughter. I glared at him and he pressed his lips together, trying to swallow the laughter, but it was impossible. His whole body shook with it. My body shook with anger.

I turned to my sister. "When you learn what has been going on, Breeze, I hope you'll understand." Then I picked up Flynn's salad and dumped it on his head.

"Manager to outdoor patio," a voice on the PA said. "Manager to outdoor patio."

I glanced around quickly for an exit and realized I couldn't make it through the restaurant without coming face-to-face with the manager. Hiking up my full skirt, I climbed clumsily over the flower containers, and ran.

15

$\mathcal{I}$t's not easy to run in princess shoes. Perhaps that's why Cinderella left one behind at the ball. I was ready to ditch both in the harbor, but Breeze usually paid a lot for shoes, and I didn't want to have to dig into my camera fund farther than I already had for this disastrous evening. Of course, I knew the restaurant manager would simply put a stop to the salad dumping and escort me to the exit. It was Flynn I was running from.

I didn't stop to rest till I got to the aquarium, where I found a bench and threw myself down on it, scaring off pigeons. I wanted to bawl, but I would not let myself cry, I would not! Instead, I sat on the bench making deep sobbing-gulping noises that drew back the birds. At last I pulled out my cell phone and pressed "Home."

There was no answer, so I tried Dad's cell phone. As usual, he hadn't remembered to turn it on. I knew that a taxi from the city to Saylor Mill would be expensive, but I couldn't stay there a second longer. I nabbed a cab.

As soon as the taxi started, so did my tears. They rolled on silently till I reached home. I climbed out and was blowing my nose just as Dad's car pulled into the driveway. Dad started toward me, cradling a bucket of carryout, looking puzzled. I waited quietly for him to unlock the front door, then stepped inside.

"You're home early," he said.

"Yeah."

There was a long silence. He set the chicken on the mail table. "What should I do, Hayley? Tell me what to do, I don't know how to help."

"I don't think you can help, Dad. Right now, I just want to wash my face and chill out."

When I reached my room, I slipped out of my dress and shoes, then removed the roses from my hair. It had been so glued together with salon stuff, it took three shampoos to untangle it. At last I wrapped myself in my bathrobe and went out to the back deck.

Dad stuck his head through the door. "Want company?"

"I don't care."

"How about a buttered roll?"

I laughed a little, and he took that as a yes, bringing out his favorite comfort food and setting it on the table between us.

We sat in silence, both of us looking up at the stars. He was probably envisioning a machine headed for Pluto. I wished I was on that machine.

"Dad," I said at last, "I know this is going to sound dumb. I mean, Mom was your wife, not your girlfriend, but—but what I need to know is, after she died, how did you stop thinking about her? What I'm asking is, if you love someone, and you can't have that person, how do you get them out of your head?"

My father turned to look at me, surprised. "You don't."

"Oh *great*!"

"Honey, your mother will always be in my head and in my heart." He paused, looking back up at the stars. "But it doesn't hurt the way it used to."

"So, so how did you get it not to hurt so much?"

"Actually, you and Breeze did. I just watched you, took care of you, loved you, and somehow, without me realizing it, the healing started. I guess I learned that from your mom. She had a rough childhood, but she survived it because she always looked outward rather than in. She kept photographing others, kept focusing on others, instead of becoming dragged down by what had happened in her own life."

For a moment, I heard Flynn's voice the day we stood by Breeze's locker: *You have what's important. You have your mother's way of seeing.*

Dad nudged the plate of buttered rolls toward me. I reached for one. When I saw the look of relief on his face, I ate all three.

"There are several phone messages," he said.

I nodded, picked up the plate, and went inside. Leaning on the kitchen counter, I listened to Breeze, then Jared, ask what was wrong. Flynn didn't ask—just left his cell phone number. I deleted the messages.

Dad took the answering machine's beeping sounds as his cue to enter the kitchen. I watched him wipe down a counter that didn't need any wiping.

"I promised I would photograph the dance," I said.

He nodded quietly.

"Nobody can do that as well as me. Except," I added, "Mom could have. And she would have, no matter what. Can you take me and pick me up later?"

My father smiled. "You know it."

I pulled on my best pair of jeans and a pretty, clingy top. Leaving my hair to fall damp and wavy, I used two small clips to keep it out of my eyes, then got a sudden inspiration: a silk rose for each side. Very girly! I slipped my digital camera into my backpack, headed toward the door, then stopped.

I had dropped the silver shoes by my bureau; one stood upright, the other lay on its side. They *were* fabulous. They made my feet look fabulous. And I'd spent a lot of time painting my toenails. After stashing my sneakers in my backpack, I slipped on the princess shoes. Ready!

As Dad drove me to school, I wondered how I was going to handle my first glimpse of Flynn and Breeze. I wondered if Jared had gone dateless to the dance, and if he and Flynn smelled like salad dressing.

"Do you have your cell phone?" Dad asked, as he pulled up to the gym door.

"Yeah. Thanks a million. I'll call you when I'm done."

He gave my hand a shy squeeze, which nearly made me bawl again.

The dance committee greeted me at the door. "Yay! She's here."

"Our own paparazzi has arrived!"

The dance had been going for forty-five minutes and the gym, transformed by glittering decorations, funky palm trees, and strings of lights, was crowded with people. The first person I saw was Jenny, looking fantastic in her green dress, dancing with Gabriel. *Hey, not looking too shabby*, I thought, *way to go, Gabe!*

I saw Kathleen on the other side of the floor with a tall guy, and I thought she had finally gotten the college boyfriend to come home. Then he turned around. It was Jared's brother, the one "with more brains than muscles." *You go, girl.*

I saw Paige flitting through the crowd. I knew that sooner or later my eyes were going to light on Flynn and Breeze. I backed into a dark corner, glad for the protection of its shadows, wanting to see them before they saw me.

"Good evening, Caldwell."

"Coach!" I exclaimed. Siefert had sought out the same dark corner. "I guess you're here to keep an eye on your boys."

He nodded. "I guess you're here to take pictures."

"Yes, sir." I glanced up at the big gym clock. "Just fifteen minutes left for them."

"I have decided to give them until ten o'clock."

"Wow! That's nice of you."

"No, Caldwell, the word is *resigned*."

I nodded, and found myself smiling a little. Coach taught freshman science and always referred to his female students as Miss So-and-so. But he called me "Caldwell," the way he called Flynn "Delancy" or Jared, "Wright." I felt like part of the team.

"So I guess you need to get into the newspaper office to get your cameras," he said.

"Actually, I left the school cameras in Jared's car, so I brought my own."

"Wright's over there," he told me, with a jerk of his head.

I glanced in the direction that Coach indicated. Jared was surveying the food table as if he hadn't eaten for days. Breeze was standing next to him. I searched the area for Flynn. Then Breeze, with that bit of telepathy we have, turned in my direction, searching the crowd. When I stepped into the light, she smiled at me, then winked.

"We put the cameras in the newspaper office," Siefert continued, removing a large ring from his belt, fingering a master key. "If you lose these keys, Caldwell, it would probably be best to leave the country."

"I'll be right back with them, Coach."

I headed for the news office, wondering about the triangle of Jared, Breeze, and Flynn, hoping I wouldn't get caught in the melodrama that was sure to come. *Just focus on your pictures, Hayley*, I told myself, as I unlocked the office door.

Closing it softly behind me, I slipped the keys in my pocket and leaned back against the door. With the lights off, moonlight shone through the bank of windows on the opposite side of the room and silvered the long table where we met each week to hash out our ideas. It was comforting to be here. It was comforting to see my camera bag waiting for me on the table.

"Hello."

My heart stopped. Flynn stood up, emerging from the shadows into the bright moonlight. I stayed where I was, my back against the door. He smelled like shampoo rather than salad—he had changed his clothes.

"Can we talk?" he asked.

"Sure. Sometime," I said. "But Coach is expecting me to come right back with the keys and—"

"Coach let me in here," Flynn interrupted.

"He did?"

"Hayley," Flynn said, "I can't see your face in the shadows."

"Yes, I know that."

He laughed softly. "I would really like to see it."

"It looks the same as it usually does."

"Okay," he said. "Which of the hundred different looks that I've seen in your eyes is there now?"

I swallowed hard. He couldn't help but make me ache.

"I guess you saw that Breeze and Jared are back together," Flynn said.

"They are?" I replied, surprised. "I saw them standing

together, but . . ." My voice trailed off. "You've taken another hit for the team."

"What?"

"You let Jared have her back."

"Well, I guess you could say—"

"You kept your word, even though you've fallen in love with Breeze."

Flynn stared at me, then burst out laughing. "Oh, God. You don't get it. You really don't get it."

"How could I get anything?" I asked furiously. "Have you forgotten, I am innocent, naïve, ridiculously—"

"No, Hayley, no!" He crossed the room to me. "What you are is simply *honest*. You say what you mean. You don't play games. The fact that other people do, doesn't make you naïve—it makes anyone else who acts dishonestly, like me, an idiot."

I bit my lip. "I don't need you trying to make me feel better."

"Then can I make *myself* feel better?" he asked. "Hayley, give me a chance to explain."

I slid past him and moved toward the window, finding it easier to be in the light than so close to him in the darkness.

"When Jared asked me to play his little game with Breeze," Flynn said, "I thought it was crazy and stupid,

182

but I didn't care. My season had just ended. The hopes I had of being scouted early and getting a college offer had just gone up in smoke. And I had been dumped. I didn't care about anything. *Anything.*

"But sooner or later, I had to get a grip on things and stop feeling sorry for myself. So when Jared asked me, I told myself that if his plan helped him concentrate better on football, well, I could take, as you've put it, one more hit for the team."

He crossed the room to me. "I already knew what Breeze was like. I didn't have to worry about hurting a girl who was *the* queen of the dating game. Unfortunately, I had no idea the queen had a sister."

I stared down at my silver shoes. They shimmered in the moonlight.

"I had no idea I'd fall for her sister."

Fall for?

"The night we talked in the kitchen," he went on, "when you made it clear what you thought of me for taking Breeze to the team party—and by the way, Jared had *asked* me to—I told you that *sometimes* love was just a game. And you said to me, 'Then how are you supposed to believe someone when it *isn't?*'

"After that, how could I admit what I was doing? How was I supposed to say it was all pretend with your sister, but I was really falling for you? How could I expect you to believe me?"

Had he really said it? Falling for me?

"Hayley, everyone knows that Breeze is forever late," he continued. "I think it's written in our student handbook. Why did you think I kept showing up early? Not even on time, but early!"

"Guys do things like that when they're smitten with Breeze."

"The day she stood me up, why did you think I wanted to hang around? Did you think I was so stupid and desperate that I actually believed she would return?"

"Yes."

He laughed. "Honest as always. But wrong. There I was thinking, *Man, this is my lucky day! I've got Hayley all to myself.* And then Jared showed up, then Gabe."

"But Jared said you ended your arrangement with him because you couldn't keep pretending—because you were—you were in love with Breeze," I said, swallowing the hardest part of my sentence.

"I told him I was in love. I didn't tell him with who. Jared assumes that everyone thinks and feels what he does, so he assumed it was with Breeze." Flynn stepped closer, raising his hand, then hesitating, dropping it by his side. "Hayley, look at me. Look at me . . . please? Is it possible? Tell me I'm not alone in this."

I looked up at him and kept looking. I reached and with one finger gently traced his mouth.

Flynn lowered his head. His kiss was long and sweet.

"Hayley," he said, shivering a little, then pulling me tight against him.

"Flynn."

If you fell for
Love at First Click,
you'll go crazy for
The Boyfriend Game.

Trisha can't believe her luck when she gets the chance
to try out for the varsity soccer team. And things get
even better when she starts practicing one-on-one with
the cute new sophomore, Graham. Trisha would take the
soccer field over the dating game any day, but the more
time she spends on the field with Graham, the more she
realizes that dating might not be so bad.

If only Graham felt the same way. . . .